The Ghastly Gerty Swindle with the *Ghosts* of Hungryhouse Lane

SAM McBRATNEY

The Ghastly Gerty Swindle with the Ghosts of Hungryhouse Lane

Illustrated by Lisa Thiesing

HENRY HOLT AND COMPANY • NEW YORK

Henry Holt and Company, Inc.
Publishers since 1866
115 West 18th Street
New York, New York 10011

Henry Holt is a registered
trademark of Henry Holt and Company, Inc.

Published in Canada by Fitzhenry & Whiteside Ltd.,
195 Allstate Parkway, Markham, Ontario L3R 4T8.

Library of Congress Cataloging-in-Publication Data
McBratney, Sam.
    The ghastly Gerty swindle : with the ghosts of Hungryhouse Lane /
Sam McBratney; illustrated by Lisa Thiesing.
        p.   cm.
    Summary: While visiting their elderly friend Amy Steadings,
the rambunctious Sweet children worry that her new companion,
Gerty, will find the three ghosts who live in her attic. Sequel to
"The Ghosts of Hungryhouse Lane."
    [1. Ghosts—Fiction.]   2. England—Fiction.   I. Thiesing, Lisa,
ill.   II. Title.
PZ7.M47826Gf   1993   [Fic]—dc20   93-15825

ISBN 0-8050-2614-2
First Edition—1994
Printed in the United States of America
on acid-free paper.∞

10   9   8   7   6   5   4   3   2   1

Contents

The Ghastly Gerty Swindle with the *Ghosts* of Hungryhouse Lane

1 ...

Miss Amy and
the Sweet Kids

Amy Steadings lived with three ghosts in Hungryhouse Lane, near the quiet village of Tunwold.

Amy was getting on in years. One day she strained her hip while carrying coal and could no longer get upstairs to clean and polish the way she used to do. The time had come, Amy decided, to put an ad in the paper and get a nice lady companion to live with her.

This was not an easy advertisement to write, for Amy wanted to attract the right kind of person—someone who enjoyed country life and who wasn't afraid of . . . well, of the *unusual*.

Oh dear, she thought. This could be tricky. People sometimes behave rather strangely when they hear the word "ghost." It's not quite the same as having bats or mice.

Amy had inherited the house and its ghosts from

an old friend, and she firmly believed that it was her responsibility to look after them properly. She had never mentioned them to a living soul, so no one knew they were there—no one, that is, except for the children who had lived in the house for a few weeks before Amy took it over. Such interesting children! Their names were Zoe Sweet, Charlie Sweet and Bonnie Sweet. They hadn't been in the least dismayed to find spooks in the attic. They'd been overjoyed!

But they were *children*. And Amy was quite certain that children could be tougher than grown-ups when it came to . . . well, the *unusual*.

After some deep thinking she decided that it would be silly to mention the ghosts in her ad. Eventually she settled on a form of words that pleased her:

> Elderly lady seeks companion to help with the cleaning of seventeenth-century house, also for cooking and conversation. An interest in country life is essential for this position. Full board and weekly wage. Please apply with references to the address below.

There, thought Amy as she licked a stamp. That was quite enough information for the time being. When her new companion had settled in, perhaps the subject of the ghosts could be discussed over a cup of tea.

She placed the letter behind the mantelpiece clock for posting.

The Sweet kids (of whom Amy Steadings had just been thinking) had recently moved into a new house far away from Hungryhouse Lane.

Actually, it was more of a mansion. Many of the sixteen rooms had a telephone or a television set, and around the back there were beautiful gardens, a fine big swimming pool, and stables for five horses. The house was so new that the gardens had no grass, the pool had no water, and the stables had no horses.

The Sweet family had plenty of money. After winning a fortune in the national lottery, Mr. Sweet gave up his job, saying to his friends, "This is not going to change us at all, of course; we shall still be the same people underneath." It was lucky that he used that word "underneath," because on the surface Mr. and Mrs. Sweet changed completely, and they changed overnight. Money did not change their attitude to backgammon, however. Mr. and Mrs. Sweet were addicted to that game, and often discussed each other's play in rather heated tones.

Such a discussion was happening right now in the smallest of the three reception rooms.

"Two double fives," said Mr. Sweet. "I ask you, two blasted double fives in a row! They cost me that game, you know."

"I don't think so," said Mrs. Sweet with a superior smile. "My strategy was to block you in and that's what happened. I blocked you in."

"Strategy! Piffle!" snapped Mr. Sweet.

The door opened and their eldest daughter appeared, glowering. Zoe could glower better than anyone in the family.

"Mommy, he's juggling the pears again and dropping them violently on the kitchen floor."

"We're in the middle of backgammon, Zoe dear," said Mrs. Sweet. "What does it matter if he drops a pear or not?"

"Because they'll pick up germs. And they'll bruise and have to be thrown out, and we'll miss out on our natural fiber and vitamin C. Also, it's wasteful and an insult to hungry people in Third World countries."

Mrs. Sweet glanced meaningfully at Mr. Sweet, who sighed and cried, "Charlie! Stop juggling with the pears."

The reply came from far away. "Bonnie hid my juggling balls."

"Bonnie! Give him back his juggling balls."

"He said my doll Lulubelle picks her nose!"

Up rose Mr. Sweet, determined to nip this latest nonsense in the bud. First he gathered his children together in the hall and spoke to them firmly—Zoe, Charlie, Bonnie (nursing Lulubelle) and Muldoon, the dog.

"Now listen. Nobody can concentrate with that

racket going on. If it continues, there will be no swimming pool. It will sit there empty, without water, forever. Now go and watch TV or read the *Encyclopedia Britannica*."

Off he marched with long and energetic strides—the walk of a man who meant every word he said. But Mr. Sweet did not know that Charlie and Bonnie liked the pool empty (it made a jolly good sunken tennis court). Zoe didn't want to swim either—she had plans to turn the pool into a national hospital for sick seals and dolphins. However, they were quiet until after lunch.

The next row broke out when Charlie pointed the TV remote control at Lulubelle and said, "Zap-zap-zap-zap-zap."

"Stop it!" cried Bonnie, shielding Lulubelle with her arms.

"Stop what?"

"You're switching her off! You did it before and you're doing it again."

"Where are my juggling balls, then?"

The juggling balls were hiding up a drainpipe in the garden, but Bonnie had no intention of ever telling where they were after Charlie had said at breakfast that Lulubelle picked her nose. She hadn't forgotten those words and she never would forget. The bashed-up, bald-headed ragdoll had survived four birthday parties, but looked about a hundred and three in spite of the brand-new pink satin bows it wore.

Around came the remote control again. Zap!

"MOMMEEE!"

"What is it now?"

"Mommy, he's switching off Lulubelle. He's switching off my Lulubelle with the remote control."

The excitement in the air made Muldoon howl as if the postman was coming. (He hated the postman with all his heart.) Meanwhile, Charlie had accidentally switched channels, so that Zoe, instead of watching her nature program, saw Popeye swallowing spinach and then beating up Bluto.

"Mommy! The swine is channel-hopping again and I should have been an only *child*!"

Into this din rushed Mr. Sweet with the light of battle flashing in his eyes. "You—up to your room. You—find those juggling balls. You—do the dishes. Into your bed, dog!"

He watched them all go, then returned to the other room, where he sat at the backgammon board for some moments as if to marvel at the silence.

"Geoffrey."

"Yes, dear?"

"Wouldn't it be a good idea if we sent the children away for a holiday?"

Mr. Sweet knew what his wife meant. They could both do with a break. But who in their right mind would take them? He rolled his dice and got blasted double fives *again*.

* * *

Later that day the Sweet kids (including Muldoon) met on the bottom of the empty swimming pool to hear Zoe read the letter they had just received in the mail. It was from Amy Steadings, their friend in Hungryhouse Lane:

> Dear Zoe, Charlie and Bonnie,
>
> How are you all? It's so nice to be writing to you again. When are you coming to visit me, I'd like to know? Soon, I hope, now that the holidays have started. From your last letter, Zoe, I see that you are doing a project on ghosts. I wonder what your teacher will make of it! How is the juggling, Charlie? I'm sure you'll soon be good enough to join a circus. Bonnie, did you get the satin bows I sent for Lulubelle?

At this point Bonnie nodded her head, and said "Yes."

> I have taken a lady companion. I'm not so sure that she is suitable, but time will tell. I shall ask her to stay out of the attic for the time being. I'm sure you can all guess why. I haven't seen Lady Cordelia or Sir James for some months. Nor little Bobbie either, of course. I can't get up there now because of my bad hip.
>
> All my love,
> Amy.
>
> P.S., I shall write to your parents and *make* them bring you!

Zoe folded the letter and tucked it under Muldoon's collar. No one spoke for some time, for that letter had brought back quite a few memories of the house in Hungryhouse Lane. Zoe remembered Lady Cordelia McIntyre floating down through the ceiling in her wonderful Cinderella dress. Charlie thought of Bobbie, the shabby little chimney-sweep ghost in bare feet. Bonnie Sweet remembered the night she threw Lulubelle at Sir James, the ghost with the sword and the wig. Lulubelle had gone right through him!

"Well?" said Zoe. "Do we want to go or not? I could interview those spooks for my school project. Yes, I think we might go. What about you, Charlie?"

Charlie thought it over. For his birthday he'd been given a hand-held tape recorder instead of the unicycle and juggling clubs he'd asked for. It might be interesting, he reckoned, to make tapes of sheep sounds and cow sounds and ghost sounds.

Bonnie wasn't sure. "We would like to go," she said, referring to herself and Lulubelle, "but I don't think she's got a VCR."

"What about you, Smelly?" Zoe asked Muldoon.

Pleased to get a mention, Muldoon performed a twirl or two and appeared to bark "Yes."

2...

Gertrude "Elizabeth" Moag

"Mmm," Gertrude Moag said to herself when she saw the ad. "Lady companion, eh? Seventeenth-century house, if you please, oh la-di-dah! Now, that sounds a bit promising, Gerty, my love."

But do you like the country, Gerty? she asked herself. And the answer was no. How could you like something that was so empty, wide and green? Not that she minded the odd hanging basket or even a window box with a few pansies in it; but the thought of wearing rubber boots made Gerty's poor toes curl up in horror.

Still, it would do no harm to take a look at the place. She set to one side the woolly sweater she was knitting for her only son and fetched some writing paper. To get the job, she needed a reference. *Gertrude Elizabeth Moag* (she wrote)

> *has worked for me for many years, and I found her to be a caring, friendly person of the kind*

you just can't find nowadays no matter where you look—her sort don't grow on trees, I can tell you.

Children? She was marvelous with my children, and she made life so wonderful for my elderly mother with her home cooking. You cannot imagine how we all bawled and cried when she left us; it was awful. I, Lady Diana Rich, envy her next employer greatly and recommend her with all my power.

Lady Diana Rich

In this letter that Gerty wrote for herself, some things were not quite true. She didn't know a Lady Diana Rich. Neither did she have a middle name, but "Elizabeth" had such a nice ring to it—it made her feel . . . well, Elizabethan.

On the other hand, she *had* once been a sort of nanny to a bad little boy who wouldn't go to bed at night. Gerty had sorted out the little monster by putting his hamster in the trash can every time he misbehaved. *That* soon had him skipping up the stairs to say his prayers. The parents found out about this, though, and fired her. (Parents were far too soft these days, Gerty often said.)

In her next job, an antique Chinese vase had been found in her wardrobe. That was bad enough, but it had also been wrapped up in her summer petticoat. All very embarrassing. Difficult to explain. Oh well,

Gerty sighed as she packed for the morning train to Tunwold village, it was all water under the bridge.

And what a dreary place Tunwold village turned out to be, with its one wide street! It felt like the middle of bleeping nowhere. Then she had to walk two miles along a country road, with aching bunions, until she arrived at Hungryhouse Lane. An avenue of massive trees led up to the old house, and birds sang out as she crunched along the gravel path below.

Birdsong! thought Gerty. Anybody who thinks that's singing needs their head looked at.

Well, what a house! It seemed at first to be all roof—the thatch was so neat that a hairdresser might have given it the old back and sides only yesterday, especially up there where it curled over two small attic windows. Curiously like eyes, those windows . . . Wouldn't be surprised if that old straw leaks, thought Gerty. And as for those plants creeping up the walls, why, you might just as well put up a ladder for spiders and earwigs. And worse. Should have packed a mousetrap, thought Gerty.

But this was a grand place, no doubt. *Time passes slowly here*, the old house seemed to say. *I've had three hundred years already, and three hundred more to come.* Gerty was no fool. She'd seen such places in the glossy magazines. Whoever lived here had money, lovely money. . . .

The old lady who came to the door wore a brooch

at her throat and her hair in a bun. Also two cardigan sweaters. Probably felt the cold. Deep and quiet eyes, both somewhat red and dull. Genteel sort, Gerty guessed. Easy meat.

"How are you, dear? I've come about your ad in the paper. Gertrude Elizabeth Moag is my name. I've had lots of experience. Got a bit of leg trouble have we, yes? I can tell. Been a nurse in my time, of course. Your house is a picture, dear, I'm sure I've seen it in a painting—and the little birds singing in the trees! The countryside is just so pretty, don't you think?"

A blink or two. Then, "Oh . . . well . . . I must say, I did think applicants would phone me first, Miss Moag."

"*Mrs.*, dear. Phones!" Gerty dismissed all phones with a sweep of her hand. "What do phones tell you, I always say. Here's my reference." And here, Gertrude Elizabeth Moag lowered her voice. "Lady Diana Rich. Her cousin was twenty-second in line, you know."

"I beg your pardon?" said Amy Steadings.

"In line for the throne, dear. The *throne.*"

They came into the hall. And ooh, what a flight of stairs, how they seemed to soar before disappearing round a bend! A grandfather clock of classic proportions looked down from the first landing. On the way through to the kitchen Gerty peeped into the parlor, feasting her roving eyes on an actual Persian carpet

on the floor. None of your pretend reproduction rub-
bish here!

In the kitchen lots of ancient copper things hung
on the walls. And ornamental plates. The huge black
Aga cookstove gave out a heat she could feel from
here. A few dishes and some washing lay about.

"We'll soon have it looking the way it should be,"
said Gerty, folding a tea cloth.

"But I quite like it the way it is."

"Of course! Things should look lived in, shouldn't
they, dear? A little crumple is comfortable, I always
say. Why don't you sit down and we can talk things
over while I make us a nice cup of tea?"

Later that day Gerty unpacked her bags in an upstairs room with white and lemon walls—nice and
light and bright. A tapping on the window made her
jump, but it was only a branch of creeping ivy moving
with the breeze. Gerty made short work of it with a
pair of nail scissors, then set out a large book on the
table beside her: *Antiques and How to Recognize
Them.* It was her favorite book and she read it every
day.

In the kitchen far below, Amy Steadings was not
quite sure what to make of Gertrude Elizabeth Moag.
The woman seemed to be a little common, and perhaps even coarse; but she didn't seem to be the nervous sort, and that might be very important. In any
case, Amy liked to think the best of people—this had

been her policy throughout life and it had served her very well. Besides, no one else had applied for the position of companion. She would make a point of telling Gertrude to stay out of the attic for the time being.

3...

A Bandage for Bonnie

When Mrs. Sweet read the letter from Amy Steadings in Hungryhouse Lane, for some moments she didn't quite know what to make of it.

Here was someone who actually wanted her three children to come and stay for a few days? All of them—together? Good heavens, what a surprise. Not that they were terribly wicked children, but they certainly weren't perfect. Most of their uncles and aunts liked to be told in advance that they were coming so that ornaments and breakable things could be removed to a safe place.

Zoe Sweet, like many eldest children, was a rather bossy sort. It was as if she'd said to herself, "Right, I've been born first and I'm going to make the most of it." She believed strongly that her mother and father didn't understand that children have rights. Take the pear incident, for example. People had the right to eat unbruised pears, and Mother should have banned Charlie from eating pears for two years so that he would learn his lesson and never juggle pears again. Zoe got top marks in many of her tests at school, and was very interested in first aid.

Charlie, the middle Sweet, was a moody boy who gave a lot of trouble to his sisters. Only yesterday he played them a recording of them snoring their heads off in bed. (The sound was actually water sucking down the plug hole, but it still drove them crazy.) From time to time Charlie developed a passion for something. He would suddenly take up bone collecting, and just as suddenly give it up for airplane spotting or juggling. While his big sister believed in rights, Charlie believed in grabbing what you could get. He didn't mind eating bruised pears. Or even no pears. He could easily buy himself a whole bag of pears and gobble them all by himself in a corner of the swimming pool. At school he was good at math but bad at spelling, although this did not worry him because he now planned to work in sound effects when he grew up.

Little Bonnie was so sweet that she melted the hearts of people in supermarkets. However, those familiar with her will of iron and her loud screams were not fooled. (Bonnie was quite likely to refuse pears and scream for melon boats with little umbrellas sticking out of them.) Mr. Sweet usually picked her up by the heels and set her in the bath when she had one of her tantrums. Her doll Lulubelle had no mouth. Bonnie had taken off the red-thread smile in a temper because Lulubelle kept on smiling when she, Bonnie, was unhappy. When big, she expected to work at wrapping things up nicely in shops because she could now tie lovely satin bows.

Muldoon Sweet licked Charlie's feet when he hung them out of bed at night; acted as a horse for Lulubelle; and sat up and begged for Zoe when nobody else would obey her orders. He regarded himself as one of the Sweet kids and refused to eat dog food.

"Geoffrey," said Mrs. Sweet. "Look at this. Amy Steadings has invited the children down to stay with her for a few days in the country. Isn't that awfully nice of her?"

Geoffrey Sweet put down his *Financial Times* to accept the letter from his wife. "Well, I'm bound to say that she seems very fond of them for some reason," he agreed with a frown. "How curious. Perhaps the poor woman is lonely, although I see that she has taken a lady companion."

Just then the Sweet parents heard an almighty scream coming from the hall. It was the sort of sound that makes you want to rush and see what awful thing has happened, and yet somehow roots you to the spot because you are terrified of what you might see when you get there. Mr. Sweet threw away his

Financial Times and tried not to panic. Mrs. Sweet, therefore, made it into the hall before him.

The sight that met her eyes made her poor heart lurch. Little Bonnie lay stretched out at the bottom of the stairs, in a small pool of blood, unconscious to the world. As Mr. Sweet arrived, Zoe was already wrapping the little blond head in a red-stained bandage, saying into Charlie's tape recorder, "Home accidents account for some thirteen percent of fatalities every year."

From the third step up, Muldoon pointed his nose at the roof and just howled as if he could smell the postman.

"Geoffrey, she's fallen down the stairs! She may have broken her neck!"

While the appalled parents looked on, Zoe ever so slowly straightened a Bonnie leg. "This will obviously need splints."

"Leave her *alone*, Zoe!" cried Mrs. Sweet, while Mr. Sweet rushed to the phone and seized it with hands that trembled.

Bonnie sat up. Zoe flew into a rage.

"Daddy, you are ruining *everything*."

"It's only pretend," said Bonnie. "Was I good?" Then she licked some of the tomato sauce.

Mrs. Sweet sank onto the third step up beside the howling Muldoon. Her husband replaced the phone with a blank look on his face. He would have a thing

or two to say in a moment, but not yet. Right now he was speechless.

"She didn't fall down the stairs?" said Mrs. Sweet.

"No! And how am I supposed to get first-aid practice if people are always butting in?"

"Practice?" Mrs. Sweet stared at the open first-aid kit. "Couldn't you have told us? Couldn't you have . . . warned us?"

"People don't get warnings about accidents, Mother. And I sincerely hope that you aren't going to complain about the sauce, because I have to get used to the sight of blood. Everybody thinks it's a joke, but it's not a joke and you won't be laughing if I save somebody's life one day."

Nobody was laughing. Mr. Sweet, who looked as though he might have fallen down the stairs himself, spoke.

"You are going on holiday. Tomorrow. I shall phone Amy Steadings tonight. In fact, I'll phone her now."

"But she hasn't got a VCR, Daddy," said Bonnie sweetly.

"We'll buy her one!" said Mr. Sweet between clenched teeth. "Go and pack."

"And who knows," said Mrs. Sweet, brightening up considerably, "if you're *very* well behaved and don't do silly things, there may be water in the swimming pool when you get back."

Then she noticed how Mr. Sweet was staring at the tomato-sauce bandage around Bonnie's head. Perhaps water in the swimming pool wasn't a good bet right now.

4 ...

Why Not the Attic?

Why *not* the attic, that's what Gerty wanted to know as she polished the banister on the first landing.

What was up there? What could be tucked away under the old straw roof that was so special and precious, eh? "There's no need for you to go into the attic for the time being, Gertrude," the old lady had said.

So what secret was she hiding? Something wonderful or something dreadful? Or something priceless like a painting by an old Dutch master? Of course Gerty wanted to find out what was up there. Any normal person would!

As Gerty caressed the face of the grandfather clock with her cloth, she seemed to love her work. Even after a hundred years and more of ticking and tocking away the lonely days, its walnut still took ever such a lovely shine. "Fit for a queen, you are," she told it.

Oh yes, Gerty loved that clock very much indeed. Would it fit into a van, though, she wondered?

Now she moved up to the second landing, just four bare wooden stairs away from the tiny attic door. Maybe it was dangerous in there, and Amy Steadings wanted her to keep out for her own good.

So just be careful, Gerty!

The door opened. She peered into the gloom. Her hand fell upon a switch—good. Light flooded the room, and her eyes lit up like a pair of freshly minted coins.

Over there she saw wartime gas masks and old books; over here brown photographs in silver frames lying in an ancient baby carriage with solid rubber tires. Oh my, goodies galore! Wasn't it strange how one person's junk became another person's fortune? There were rolled-up rugs, frightful paintings (but with lovely frames), an elephant's foot, a huge glass bottle called a carboy in Gerty's book of antiques (twice as big as a balloon), sets of cigarette cards (showing Hollywood movie stars of the forties and fifties), a Hornby train hardly out of its box—and strike me pink with a yard brush, thought Gerty, there's a fine old spinning wheel leaning against the chimney. And a rocking chair! On the rocking chair she found twelve perfect little lead soldiers. Musketeers, by the look of them, and worth a bleeping penny or two to the right collector. Pausing only to thrust the box of soldiers into her apron pocket, Gerty crawled out of the attic backward and put out the light.

At that moment—the moment of switching out the light—something curious happened. In the sudden gloom Gerty thought she saw a kind of afterglow with an almost human shape, a dusty sprinkling of light that seemed to evaporate even as she stared through it; then it was gone.

"How funny peculiar," Gerty muttered as she blinked her eyes. "I'll be needing my glasses for cleaning, soon."

On the first landing she opened the grandfather clock and set the box of soldiers inside. There wasn't much room in there beside the flintlock gun and the bone china figurines by Durkheim. (Gerty had been collecting already.)

Downstairs, after checking that her employer was occupied elsewhere, Gerty phoned a London number.

"Now, listen carefully because I have to talk soft. The place is a paradise, you have no idea. Yes. I couldn't even start to make a list of the goodies: china, lead soldiers, clocks, you name it and it's here, ducky. When? The sooner the better—I'll let you know. Is your cold better? Well, rub that chest with oil of eucalyptus! And don't you dare go out without an undershirt."

Gerty went into the kitchen, saying, "There we are, not a speck of nasty old dust in sight. I've just left the vacuum up there, dear, to save all the bother of hauling it up the stairs tomorrow."

Frowning, Amy Steadings plucked a few strands

of spider's silk from Gerty's skirt. "What on earth have you been doing with yourself? You're covered in cobwebs."

"Coffee, dear?" Careless of you, Gerty, she was thinking. "Or tea?"

"You haven't been into the attic, Gertrude?"

"Not unless you mean that little door at the top of the house. Thought there might be something in there that needed cleaning, didn't I? Well, such a mess! You won't be wanting *that* cleaned up, will you, dear? I don't think I could face it."

"You didn't . . . see anything?"

"Only a lot of old junk," said Gerty sharply. "Now, I don't know about you, but personally I am gasping for a good strong cup of hot tea."

What Gertrude Moag had almost seen upstairs was the ghost of Lady Cordelia McIntyre, who really had no idea what that person with the terribly strong-looking arms was doing in Amy Steadings's attic. Amy never allowed strangers up here—certainly not without first warning Cordelia that they might be coming.

Or was this the new companion whom Amy had talked about getting? Very likely. The lady had an apron on; and she wore, besides, the most ghastly cloth around her head that Cordelia had ever seen.

Fascinated—and with her Presence hidden in a

pool of light—Cordelia watched this new person smile and nod as she picked up one object after another, often smoothing away the dust with a loving hand. Good gracious, she even talked to herself. And then, after popping a box of toy soldiers into her apron pocket, she crawled out of the attic and switched off the light.

How very odd, thought Cordelia, allowing her Presence to drift through the floor until she came to the first landing. Here she used another ghostly trick of light to observe something odder still: The new person opened the front of the grandfather clock and placed the box of soldiers inside.

Cordelia returned to the attic, where she fiddled anxiously with the phantom jewelry around her neck. Even after all these years as a ghost she was still a little nervous of uncertainty and change.

Her husband had been with Lord Clive in old India. One day, as she bathed a scab behind her elephant's ear, the grateful beast had patted her with its trunk and finished her on the spot. Like most ghosts, Cordelia was a quiet soul whose only ambition was to enjoy long periods of Unwakeful Serenity*—she had no time at all for that clanking of chains and wailing in the night that a small minority of ghosts

---

* This is a ghostly condition—you may like to think of Unwakeful Serenity as a kind of hibernation.

seemed to go in for, and indeed she had not "materialized" for six months or more.

Should she waken her two companions, she wondered? Her companions were Bobbie, the little ghost who lived in the chimney, and Sir James Walsingham, who lived in the carboy. They would want to be told about strangers in the house. . . .

Perhaps not, Cordelia decided. After all, poor little Bobbie couldn't speak a word after choking to death during a fall of soot over a hundred and fifty years ago. And as for James, *he* was such a vague and grumpy sort, and so full of grand ideas, that one could never guess what he would do next. He had become an ex-human being about 1758. Among other things, he claimed that he and Mozart had once dined on the earth's last dodo under the biggest chandelier in Europe.

There was no need to waken James, Cordelia now saw, for he suddenly sank down from the roof at an alarming rate. Something had obviously put him into a tizzy. James always quivered when he became excited, and he was quivering now from the curls of his enormous wig to the buckles on his once-fashionable shoes. Even the lace hanky at his wrist seemed to flutter like a large moth.

"Drat and blast, Cordelia, have I got news for you! This is going to make you gnash your teeth, or I'm no Englishman! Have you seen who's coming?"

"No, James, I have not."

"To the window then, by jove."

A white and rather beautiful horseless carriage had just come to a halt at the door of the house below. Five people got out, but it was the dog that Cordelia recognized first, because it reminded her of those mongrels with which men hunted rats along the banks of the Thames long ago.

And there, too, was that little girl with the terribly loud scream. The boy got out last.

"That's him!" cried James. "That's the one. He's the bounder who put frog spawn in my carboy the last time he was here. Well, there go peace and quiet out the blasted window. Oh, for a moment of Genuine Presence, I would go down there and send them packing with a well-chosen word or two."

Cordelia sighed. She had expected this kind of exhibition from James. It was just this kind of behavior that got him into trouble in the first place. One evening long ago a mouse jumped out of his wig and caused his hostess to faint. Unfortunately, someone then accused him of being a bounder for harboring a rodent like that. Insults flew, faces were slapped and a duel was arranged. At the following dawn Sir James Walsingham was shot through the heart and became an ex-human being. Two hundred years later, he still hadn't learned his lesson.

"Calm yourself, James," said Cordelia.

"I don't want to calm down. There's trouble coming. I can feel it in my bones."

"You haven't got any bones," Cordelia pointed out. "And the last time you said a few well-chosen words, as you put it, you got yourself shot. Amy is down there with them, and I am quite sure she knows what she is doing. Besides, you are being ungrateful."

With an almighty sniff, James went through the motions of taking snuff from the back of his hand. Then, with his hanky, he dusted away the snuff that hadn't gone up his nose. Old habits die hard, thought Cordelia.

"I? Ungrateful?"

"You know very well that those children did us a very great favor when they were here before. Things are often not as bad as they seem."

James allowed himself to drift into an upside-down position so that his wig rested an inch or two from the floor. He often responded to criticism in this way. If people wanted to argue with him, let them jolly well talk to his feet.

5...

The Arrival
of the Sweet Kids

Gerty could hardly believe her eyes, frankly, when the white Rolls Royce drew up at the door. A snobby great Rolls! Most of the people she knew got into a machine like that when they were off to a wedding or a funeral.

And there were more shocks in store. For a start, the dog that got out had its left hind leg in a bandage. Next came a small girl screaming, "I can tie bows, I can tie bows." Then a bigger girl, carrying a first-aid kit the size of a small suitcase. The boy seemed to have a camera, or perhaps a small tape recorder, in his hand. Suddenly every automatic window of the car zoomed down, and the mother of this lot said to the father, "You're pressing the wrong button, darling, if you want the windows *up*."

Strike me pink, what an outfit, thought Gerty. So

these were the Sweet kids. It might be a bit of a nuisance to have them snooping about, but she'd soon lick the blighters into shape.

"Oh, how lovely!" cried Amy as she spread kisses all around, including the doll. "I am so pleased. Shall we all have something to eat?"

"Oh no, we really must be going," said Mrs. Sweet. "This is so kind of you, Amy, and the children are looking forward to their stay so much. Aren't they, Geoffrey?"

"We are most grateful," Mr. Sweet said gravely as he lifted a VCR out of the trunk of the Rolls. "This is a present for you, Miss Amy."

"Oh, but I couldn't . . ."

"But you *must*," cried Mrs Sweet. "It'll keep them . . . occupied. We have warned them to be good."

"If we're not good, you're going to fill in our new swimming pool with great big ugly stones, aren't you, Daddy?" piped up the smallest Sweet, but no one seemed in a hurry to answer her.

Amy turned, smiling. "I must remember my manners! Allow me to introduce my new companion, Mrs. Gertrude Moag."

"How do you do, Mrs. Moag," said Mrs. Sweet. "I'm sure you'll be of great assistance to Miss Amy. You've been a governess, I believe?"

Gerty smiled as her brain whirled. Whose children

had she said she looked after? "Yes, dear, I was nanny to Sir George Leicester's triplets."

"I thought it was Lady Diana Rich."

"Hers too, of course," said Gerty without batting an eyelid. Her gaze swooped on the smallest Sweet and her doll. "I expect you'll want me to tell you the story of Snow White and the Three Dwarfs, won't you, little darling?"

"I think you probably mean seven dwarfs," said the bigger girl. "Or maybe Goldilocks and the Three Bears. Anyway, it doesn't matter. We've seen them all on video."

A wicked glance from Gerty lit on the eldest Sweet. Any more talk like that and you're going to need that first-aid kit, sweetie. Gerty smiled at the boy.

"And what do you like to do?"

"Juggle."

End of conversation. Gerty now tried to cuddle the little girl's doll, and that was when she noticed that the doll's face had no mouth. She had seen missing eyes, missing ears and missing limbs before, but this was the first mouthless doll Gerty had ever met, and she found it quite shocking.

"She doesn't like other *people,*" cried the little horror, and yanked the doll out of Gerty's hands.

With a definite narrowing of the eyes, Gertrude Moag turned to the dog. "And who is this dear little fellow? Who's a nice doggy with a poor bad leg, then?"

Muldoon, whose leg was perfectly all right, rolled over on his back, thus presenting his bald, pink, mud-caked underside.

"He wants you to scratch his belly," said Charlie.

"I'm allergic, dear," said Gertrude. "Be sure and keep it out of the kitchen."

The time had come for Mr. and Mrs. Sweet to go, which they did with many a triumphant blast of the melodious horn. Gertrude excused herself to phone her sick mother, while Amy led the Sweet kids into the kitchen.

Some people in this world have warm and lovely natures—they actually listen to what others have to say and are genuinely interested in what other people do. Amy Steadings was one of them. Bonnie had no trouble with allowing Lulubelle onto Miss Amy's knee; indeed, she even agreed that Amy should get out her needle there and then and sew a nice smiley-mouth onto her orange face. Then the sewing had to stop, for Zoe hung Miss Amy's arm in a sling to demonstrate her skills.

"It's just like you to take up first aid, Zoe. I'm sure you'll save someone's life one day."

She insisted on seeing Charlie's juggling, even though his juggling balls were still soggy after a week up the drainpipe in the garden. He managed to get to two hundred and four before dropping one.

"That's wonderful, Charlie. I don't know anyone who can juggle like that."

Charlie, who wasn't used to praise, glowed in spite of himself.

"Can we see the spooks?" asked Zoe. "I have to interview them for my school project."

"Tomorrow." Miss Amy lowered her voice. "I'll arrange an interview for ten thirty in the attic. And afterward we'll have a picnic in the pond field. I have ever so many frogs this year, Charlie."

I'll tape one if it croaks, thought Charlie.

That night a shifting gray shape floated down through two ceilings as far as the first landing, where it took on the airs and graces of Sir James Montgomery Walsingham.

Sir James spent most of his time sleeping—or, to be accurate, in a state of Unwakeful Serenity—but on wide-awake nights like this one he liked to get out of the attic and see a bit of the world. Going for a float, he called it. Sometimes he slid down the banister on his wig. Sometimes he even drew his sword and fought one of the velvet curtains to the death. Of course, he wouldn't have been caught dead doing any of these things by Cordelia or that lower-class chimney ghost; but such little moments made life interesting.

If "life" was the right word, James thought glumly. Nowadays a chap didn't have enough muscle to turn the pages of a book, thanks to that blasted rodent long ago.

Then he heard a noise. It almost scared his sword out of its scabbard. However, looking along the corridor, he saw that it was only that Gertrude person, the new servant, applying a bit of the old spit and polish to the ornaments in an alcove.

Somewhere a clock struck the hour after midnight. What a chance this was to put the wind up her, good and proper! Perhaps he could rise up out of the floorboards and ask her would she like a pinch of snuff. Or he could pretend that she'd just tickled him with her duster. Nothing like a laughing ghost to turn people a nice shade of off-white.

But these were fantasies, James knew. Amy Steadings was a stick-in-the-mud about that sort of light entertainment. She had once threatened to put James and his carboy down a well just for frightening some window-cleaning chap off his ladder.

Drifting to the ground floor, James saw the Moag woman go to the telephone. Devilish contraption. He didn't trust it. In his day if you wanted to speak to a chap you called for your carriage and went round to see him.

"Make it tomorrow afternoon," she said quietly. "They're all going for a picnic."

James toyed with the idea of staring out at her from a mirror (just a *little* fright); but then, thinking that it wasn't worth it, he levitated toward the attic.

Cordelia was talking to that chimney sweep, Bobbie, who had died up a chimney in Manchester in

1831. Bobbie was a girl, though a fellow would never guess as much from the cropped hair and the rags she wore. Not to mention the bare feet. And those blasted brushes she carried everywhere. Naturally James was sorry that she'd had such a hard life, but why couldn't she have been a ghost from good society? Not that he was a snob by any means—but a chimney sweep, dash it all! The girl never said a word—*couldn't* say a word—and if there was anything James liked, it was a little cultured conversation like his own.

"I say, Cordelia, what a worker that woman is. Imagine polishing brasses and vases at this time of night, what? She's actually taken a picture off the wall to dust behind it. Every spider in the house must be shaking in its boots, I can tell you." Here, James paused to glare at the brushes on Bobbie's shoulder. "Why don't you take the hint, girl? Isn't there something useful you could do instead of carrying those things around all day like an extra head?"

Bobbie made a rude gesture with the brushes, which James pretended to find appalling.

"Ha! I see we've been to the school of manners. It's on a par with your tailor, by jove!"

"Stop this nonsense, James," said Cordelia. "I don't see you taking off your wig or your sword or your lace hanky, either, if it comes to that, so be sensible and listen to me. There is something very strange happening. Look at your carboy. And my Rajah's foot. They have been moved."

So they had. The assorted pile of junk near the attic door included his big glass bottle and the elephant's foot, as well as that useless old spinning wheel and an ancient set of hearth irons. Cordelia's elephant foot had been stuck into an old doll's carriage.

"A bit of spring cleaning, I expect," said James.

"You don't think that that new woman is behaving strangely, then?"

"There is nothing strange about people behaving strangely, Cordelia. The strange thing would be if people weren't behaving strangely—experience tells me so."

And James, satisfied that he had been both witty and wise, said good night, and headed (literally) for his carboy.

6...

An Interview with Spooks

I'll have toast with honey," said Bonnie at the breakfast table.

"I'll have peanut butter with crackers," said Charlie.

"And I'll have *pâté de fois gras*," said Zoe, sounding very French.

Their cook, Gertrude Moag, planted a fat-fingered hand on one hip and waved the knife with which she had been slicing tomatoes and spring onions.

"Where do you think this is, the Ritz? Eh? You'll eat what's in front of you. I have sandwiches to make for the lot of you. You're going on a picnic this afternoon, remember? And you"—she meant Charlie—"if you're going to juggle, do it with one apple. Put two of those back in the dish. And what is that clipboard doing on the table, young lady?"

"I am conducting an interview at ten thirty," Zoe replied very stiffly, "and Charlie is allowed to juggle with three pears back home."

At that moment the door opened and in sauntered Muldoon with his leg (a different leg) in a beautiful bandage. He may have been heading under the table, for experience had taught him that this was a good place to pick up scraps, but he never made it.

"Beat it, fleabag!"

He was a coward, Muldoon. Through the door he streaked, a flash of white bandage.

"You might have hurt his feelings, you know," said Zoe. "And if we are having only Shredded Wheat, I want mine with warm milk."

"It's the summertime, sweetie," said Gertrude Moag.

Bonnie couldn't help staring up at her with large eyes. Who was this person who shouted at Muldoon and called people sweetie and made Charlie juggle with just one apple? If she was supposed to be a governess, she didn't look a bit like Julie Andrews in *The Sound of Music*—she was far more like the wicked stepmothers Bonnie had read about in books.

"If it's the summertime," Zoe retorted, "it's warm enough to eat cold Shredded Wheat in the garden." And so saying, she led the Sweet kids through the back door. They sat on some logs near a clump of lupins, for the weak morning sunshine had not yet dried up the dew on the grass.

They finished breakfast in silence while Charlie taped one of the local grasshoppers. Zoe found herself wondering whether she would give first aid to that terrible woman if the big knife slipped and she sliced up her finger instead of an onion. Probably she would—first-aiders couldn't pick and choose like that; it wouldn't be right. They had to save life in all circumstances. She'd certainly ask Gertrude Moag to pay for the bandages afterward, though.

"Zoe," whispered Bonnie, "do you think she's a wicked stepmother?"

"No. It's more likely that she worked for a long time in a prison for bad people. Pass me my clipboard please, Bonnie."

After Charlie had taped Muldoon slurping up cold leftover Shredded Wheat milk, they all headed for the attic.

The Sweet children had many faults, of course, but being nervous was not one of them. They were not afraid of deep dark holes in the corners of bedrooms, nor did they hide under the covers when things went bump in the night. Besides, they had met Lady Cordelia and Sir James and little Bobbie before; and so, when they entered the attic that morning, they might just as well have been visiting three odd but distant relatives.

"Hi," said Zoe. "I've got some questions here. We do projects in school nowadays. It's part of our education, okay?"

Lady Cordelia glowed under the skylight like the seed head of a dandelion. Sir James leaned to one side, as always, with his hanky hand on the hilt of his sword. (Maybe he was a bit heavier on the sword side, Charlie thought.) Bonnie stared at Bobbie. This sad little ghost, who had been used as a human brush, was the one she liked best, although not well enough to let her hold Lulubelle. Bonnie couldn't remember whether a ghost *could* hold Lulubelle.

"We are so pleased to see you again," said Lady Cordelia. "Aren't we, James? And I know that Bobbie is too."

Bobbie waved her brushes, but Sir James wore his bounder-who-put-frog-spawn-in-my-carboy expression as he said, "I'm not so sure about this interview. People in our position don't like publicity—Unwakeful Serenity and all that. The fewer people who know about us, the better."

"You needn't worry," said Zoe. "I'll not mention your names. I'll just call you Spooks One, Two and Three."

"Hang on a minute," said Charlie.

He had preparations to make. From his little recorder he removed his tape of country sounds and replaced it with a fresh one. "Spook interview, side one. Recording engineer, Charlie Sweet." He glanced up at the three curious ghosts. "Right, you're on. And don't mumble."

"Must you call me a *spook*?" asked James. "I'm a Nonmaterial Presence, if you must refer to me at all!"

It really was a very fine interview—Zoe was sure that her topic would beat every other one out of sight and make people jealous of her. The only problem was that Cordelia said such interesting things about being a ghost that Zoe forgot to write some of them down. For once Charlie's sound-recording skills were coming in useful.

"There is a sadness about all ghosts," she said, smoothing her insubstantial dress with weightless hands. "Imagine being a ghost at a party. You can't dance, can't eat the lovely food, can't make eyes at someone with wonderful manners and a splendid title—he would be sure to run away if you did! And of course, you can't open presents. If you are a ghost, you are the way you are. You may be able to float through windows or melt into walls, but what use are skills like these when you can never dance a minuet under glittering chandeliers, or wear the latest fashions? No. One's hairdo is forever, I'm afraid."

There was such a deep silence in the attic when Cordelia finished her reflections that she became quite embarrassed. "Gracious me, I didn't mean to sound so depressing! Let's talk about something more interesting. Did you get the lead soldiers?"

"What lead soldiers?" asked Charlie.

"The ones Miss Amy's new companion put inside the grandfather clock. I thought it was a strange thing to do, but then you children arrived."

"She put them into the *clock?*" said Charlie.

"Yes. I assume she means to give them to you in case you are bored."

Bonnie wanted to know more about the spooks. "What color is your toothbrush?" she asked James, who glared at her down the outline of his long nose.

"What color is my *what?*"

"He hasn't got a toothbrush," said Charlie. "He's like Lulubelle."

"Lulubelle uses mine!" cried Bonnie.

"She doesn't. She has no teeth. She didn't even have a mouth until yesterday."

"You are not allowed to say things to me," screamed Bonnie.

"I am if they're true. She can't use a toothbrush and she can't wash her face and she can't comb her hair and she never uses toilet paper."

This was too much. The huge eyes that melted the hearts of strangers in the street now seemed to light up with an inner fury as Bonnie forgot where she was.

"Mommy, he's saying things, he's saying things, he says Lulubelle never uses toilet paper!"

Even Lulubelle went berserk and belted Charlie on the jaw, while Muldoon chose to howl in sympathy. The noise was so awful that the little sweep put her hands over her ears and melted through the chimney wall—brushes and all.

"Stop it, stop it!" Zoe yelled above them all. "They'll fill in the swimming pool, they'll fill in the swimming pool, and we need it for sick dolphins!"

Good gracious me, Cordelia said to herself. It was quite beyond her understanding how three children and a dog could suddenly make such an unbelievable noise. She looked around for James—just in time to see his feet disappearing through the roof.

Madness, thought James. Mayhem and utter madness! Was there peace anywhere on Earth—was it true what Amy Steadings had said, could a fellow nowadays go to the moon?

Fortunately it was a calm day outside, and by taking reasonable precautions he made it to the hayloft. There was a plague of blasted mice in the hayloft, of course, but right now he regarded the beasts as the lesser of two evils. They only squeaked.

Toothbrushes and toilet paper. Modern inventions! If that's progress, thought James, you can jolly well hang me in the morning. "Time is my enemy," he cried, while drawing his sword in a way that helped him to relieve his feelings. "Time itself! Why don't they learn how to stop time instead of pussyfooting about with toothbrushes and toilet paper? Now, *that* would be progress!"

After some minutes of prancing about in the hayloft, he returned to the house, fearful that a storm

might come up and leave him stranded among mice. On easing his Presence through a landing window, he saw something that made him pause for a pinch of imaginary snuff. The youngest of the three horrors was fiddling with the door of the grandfather clock.

What was she up to now? How nice it would be, thought James, if the door closed and the clock somehow ate her. This thought, and the snuff, made him feel more like himself as he levitated toward the attic.

7...

Tongue Sandwiches

Although it was half past twelve in the middle of the day, Bonnie sneaked along the first landing like a thief in the night. She had Lulubelle with her. Hidden down the front of her jogging suit she also had Charlie's juggling balls.

She had things to do. Important things. And she didn't want anybody to see her doing them, because that would spoil her special plan to pay Charlie back for being beastly to Lulubelle.

The list of Charlie's crimes against Lulubelle was now too long to be ignored. Last week at bathtime he'd said she wanted to marry a duck, and he had also made her float in the soap dish with a sign around her neck saying SHARK BAIT. And how dare he say that she never used toilet paper! He was getting far too fresh, and Bonnie knew just what to do about that.

With a quick dart she made it to the door of the grandfather clock. Her second favorite ghost—the one dressed like Cinderella at the ball when the clock struck twelve and she had to run away leaving the sad prince holding her lovely little sparkling slipper—had given her a wonderful idea for a hiding place. Imagine a clock with a door! Even her teacher at school didn't know that clocks had doors—she would certainly have told Bonnie if she did.

For just a quick shivery moment, Bonnie had the funniest feeling that someone was watching her, so she checked again that all was clear before opening the clock to pop the balls inside. Charlie would never guess!

There wasn't much room in there. The big swingy brass thing had been tied to one side to make space for lots of other objects, including a gun that looked like a trumpet. Bonnie tiptoed away from the clock as carefully as she had arrived.

Twenty minutes later the clock on the landing had another visitor. Charlie, too, remembered what Lady Cordelia had said that morning, and his curiosity had been aroused for three reasons: One, he wanted to tape the clock ticking; two, he wanted to see the lead soldiers; and three, he just wanted to look in and see clock guts.

But when he arrived, the clock had stopped ticking. As he discovered on opening the door, this was because the pendulum had been tied up. And the lead soldiers couldn't be seen under a pile of other things—including his own juggling balls.

There was no mystery here for Charlie. He knew how those balls had gotten there. He knew why, and he knew by whom.

Okay. So she wanted to play rough.

He went looking for Lulubelle.

Down in the kitchen Gerty glanced anxiously at her watch as she wrapped up the egg-salad sandwiches, and then the tongue ones. It was getting late. How in the name of goodness did it take them so long to get organized for a stupid picnic?

"Eew. I'm not eating tongue sandwiches," said the littlest Sweet. "How can the moo-cow say moo if it hasn't got its tongue?"

"Look, the cow is *dead*," snapped Gerty. "Somebody somewhere else in the world is eating the rest of it. You might as well say how does a sheep walk if we roast a leg of lamb."

String me up, thought Gerty. For breakfast they'd gobbled down bacon and *pâté de fois gras,* and they had the nerve to turn up their noses at tongue sandwiches!

"You didn't whack the crusts off," said Charlie.

"And I like my sandwiches cut into equilateral triangles, actually," said Zoe.

"Oh, please excuse me," cried Gerty. "I didn't know you needed geometry lessons to make proper sandwiches."

A distant cloud seen through the window made

her even more impatient. What if it rained and they cancelled the picnic? As Amy Steadings struggled into the room with a green blanket, Gerty clapped her hands in a let's-be-busy way.

"If you don't all hurry up, it's going to rain. Come along now; the grass will be wet and horrible and you'll have to eat your picnic standing up. Off you go!"

"What are we going to drink?" asked Zoe.

"The lemonade is in the fridge. Fetch it like a good girl, if you can carry it, that is—do you really have to bring your first-aid case to a *picnic*?"

"Of course. Someone might rip their flesh on barbed wire."

"Oh, my gawd, charming," muttered Gerty.

When Zoe opened the fridge door, she saw a plate of tongue sandwiches sitting on the second shelf. They were bound in plastic wrap and they had been sprinkled over with heads of fresh parsley. That wasn't all. They had been cut into neat equilateral triangles.

Huh, thought Zoe.

Muldoon led the picnic party out of the front door. Then, on her cane, came Miss Amy, who was helped by Zoe, who passed her first-aid case to Charlie, who passed the plastic cups to Bonnie so that he could have one hand free to tape interesting sounds if he heard any. And so Bonnie couldn't run back for Lulubelle because her arms were too full to carry anything more.

"Could you open the garden gate for us please, Gertrude," said Amy. "What are you going to do with yourself all afternoon?"

"I must walk into the village, dear. I need some stamps."

"Dear me. I'm sure I must have stamps you can have."

"Oh, stamps isn't all, duck. I've got to get a turnip and bread."

"Enjoy the tongue sandwiches," said Zoe.

"Never eat them! If I let tongue past my lips it gives me heartburn. Cheers!"

How mean could you get, Zoe thought as the picnic party moved on. Imagine making triangle sandwiches for herself and squares for everybody else! And then telling lies about it! Because if Gertrude Moag wouldn't eat those sandwiches in the fridge, who were they *for*?

Alexander the Grate

white van traveled along the highway toward Tunwold village.

It was a new van, but rather inclined to show the dust as white vehicles sometimes do. An anonymous finger had written WASH on the left rear door and ME on the right rear door. Along the side, in bold blue letters, were these words:

ALEXANDER THE GRATE
ANTIQUES AND OBJETS D'ART
OLD FIREPLACES A SPECIALITY

Alexander himself was driving on this particular day—the day of the Sweet kids' picnic. He was dressed in a leather jacket, slate-blue trousers and gray running shoes. Over the bald spot that had given him so much misery in life he wore a jaunty yachting cap. His shades had mirrors on the outside, so that when you looked at his eyes you saw two segments of reflected sky under the crescent-shaped peak of the cap. All in all, he had a sort of crumpled-but-quality look that went awfully well, he thought, with antiques.

A glance at his watch confirmed that he was on time. The plan was to arrive sometime after three and leave shortly after four with the van stuffed to the gills. He was looking forward to making a good bundle out of this trip.

Even as a child, Alexander had been very interested in other people's property. If someone in his class lost a pencil, the lost pencil had a way of being found in Alexander's schoolbag. His teacher used to say, "Now, children, Alexander only *borrowed* this pencil I found in his bag," because she was a nice person and didn't want people to think that he was a thief. She didn't even want Alexander to think that he was a thief.

Another year brought a new teacher. Somebody lost a Mickey Mouse watch and it couldn't be found anywhere, not even in Alexander's schoolbag. (Although the watch *was* in his schoolbag.) Unfortunately, little Madeline Jaffir brought tongue sandwiches to school that day. Alexander had never tasted tongue, so he swapped one of his mushy banana sandwiches for one of little Madeline's.

She nearly lost a tooth that day, because the

Mickey Mouse watch was in there, all slimy with banana. It had been a brilliant hiding place—only, Alexander's greed had let him down. Strangely enough, tongue became his favorite sandwich filling after that.

"It's those ads on TV," his mother complained to the teacher. "They'd make anybody steal, they would. I heard the Archbishop of Canterbury say so with my own ears! The poor boy sees all those lovely things he can't have."

But Alexander went on to steal other things that weren't advertised on TV—such as cases of candy sweets from supermarkets and coal from moving trucks. At sixteen years of age he was almost shot out of a tree by a bunch of furious bird-watchers for trying to rob the nest of the last osprey in the British Isles.

After the rare-egg trade, Alexander had gone into the antiques business. By buying low and selling high (and telling outrageous lies), he had managed to do quite well for himself. And of course he was prepared to commit downright robbery. Like right now.

Tunwold village was a little tucked-away place that seemed quite promising through the van window. Horse country, by the look of it. And horses meant money.

Alexander brought the van to a halt at the end of Hungryhouse Lane before getting out. Now he

needed just a little care. One must not be seen, of course. He crawled through a hole in the hedge, and from there to a shrubbery. Beyond a rose arch he watched the old lady set off on her stick with three kids and a dog. Enjoy your picnic, Alexander thought with a grin. This was going to be like taking candy from a baby—although, strangely enough, taking candy from an actual baby was one thing that Alexander had never tried. He waited just a few moments more, in case they forgot something and came back to the house, before bringing the van to the front door.

"Hello, Mom."

"Alex! Come inside, duck, I've got everything ready. How is your chest? Did you rub it with oil of eucalyptus like I told you to? A summer cold is the devil to get rid of, you know." Swinging his shades by one leg, Alexander followed his mother into the house. Silly old cow! Of course he hadn't rubbed his chest with oil of eucalyptus; the fumes would knock people off their feet. Did she think his customers had all lost their noses?

Alexander didn't speak these thoughts aloud, however. When he needed people, he could be quite charming to them, and he needed Gerty for a few months yet. One more job. Perhaps the stately home of an earl or a duke. . . .

"Nice house, Mom," he said. "Do I see a genuine

oak-beam ceiling? Man, look at that fireplace. Pity I can't take it with me. Let's load up the heavy stuff first."

"First you'll eat," said Gerty. "You can't go to work on an empty stomach."

Saying which, she set out the plate of triangular tongue sandwiches. "Your favorites, duck!"

Alexander gave her an affectionate and charming little peck on the cheek. Gerty just smiled. She was ever so pleased.

Then they went to work. The Victorian lounge-sofa was a lump of a thing, and the grandfather clock didn't exactly feel like a feather, either. Then they shifted some items from the attic, including a large and ancient bottle Gerty had wrapped in a velvet curtain for protection. The Edwardian baby carriage and the old teddy bear would certainly bring a pretty penny, thought Alexander. And the elephant's foot. No doubt about it, Mumsy-wumsy sure knew what stuff to pick.

This was the third big house they'd done in two years. Soon Alexander hoped he'd have enough cash to live the high life in some flashy spot like the Bahamas, or maybe even Rio. The climate was very good in Rio, he'd heard. No need for oil of eucalyptus there! Or Mother, either. Gerty played no part in his long-term plans.

They filled the van in thirty-five minutes.

"Are you sure they won't suspect you?" said Alexander through the window of his van.

"No. I was out all afternoon, wasn't I? Went to the village for some stamps. I'll be in touch when I've gathered up enough stuff for a second run. Two trips should do us, then I'll split. Take care now, you hear? We don't want things swishing around in the back. Half of those lovely goodies are mine, duck. I want to be comfortable in my old age."

"Don't worry about a thing," Alexander said with a sly little smile. I'll send you a postcard from Rio, he was thinking. "See you, Mom."

"And have that chest seen to," cried Gerty. "There's nothing worse than a summer cold."

It was a comfortable drive home for Alexander. He was disappointed, in a way, that he didn't even spot a policeman, for there was an odd kind of excitement in driving a van full of somebody else's property under the very nose of the law. Back at the shop, the jeweler's assistant from next door helped him to unload the goodies.

And now, on his own at last, Alexander uncovered the six stolen pictures from Hungryhouse Lane. Five of them weren't up to much—perhaps a thousand each. Nice frames. But the sixth picture had all the moody charm of a landscape by Rembrandt. Oh man, we're talking big money here, thought Alexander. Sunshine, here I come! The old magical thrill of stealing things surged once more through muscle and vein, making him lightheaded.

That was when he saw the monkey. He saw it quite plainly—the ghostly outline of a little monkey in a jacket and short trousers. And a fez. It seemed to be nibbling something. Nuts?

Well, of course, this had to be an extraordinary trick of the light. Alexander knew that it would be gone when he looked again. And so it was. He gave himself a shivery sort of shake and smiled.

You're the one who's nuts, Alex, he thought. Silly-billy!

9...

"They've Got Lulubelle . . ."

On a dry patch of ground near the top of the pond field, Amy Steadings laid out the picnic blanket and caressed its green tartan with such a long, sad sigh.

"I've always used this blanket for picnics. It doesn't seem to get old. It's the very same blanket as it always was. . . ."

The Sweet kids watched in amazement as the old lady's eyes misted over with great big wobbly tears. They had never seen a blanket make anyone cry before.

Amy attempted a recovery with a smile. "You see, my friends and I used to come here and picnic in the old days. My, but I wish I had a penny for every glass of barley water and sparkling wine that we spilled! Memory is the strangest master of all, you know. One can't choose what to remember and what to forget. There comes a time when you can't share your memories with anyone at all. Your friends and loved ones have gone. They have all gone."

Amy ended with her lower lip trembling and out of control. Without thinking, Zoe reached out and took her hand.

"We're your friends, Miss Amy," she said.

"I am your friend," Bonnie piped up. "I will always be your friend."

"I'll get out the sandwiches," Charlie mumbled.

But Amy dried her eyes on a hanky that looked very like the one on the wrist of that snooty ghost with the sword. "I'm just being so silly," she said. "And thank you very much, Charlie, but no—*I* shall prepare the picnic. You three are on your holiday, so off you go and enjoy nature while I set out all this. Don't be too long."

The Sweet kids were used to being told "Do this" and "Do that," and so were experts at thinking up reasons why they should never be asked to do anything. They seemed rather surprised that all of a sudden these skills weren't necessary. They followed Muldoon through a gap in the hedge.

It cannot honestly be said that the Sweet kids admired the shimmer of cloudy light on the running brook, or that they looked for the colorful flash of a kingfisher blue among the trees. Instead, they dive-bombed the sleeping trout with stone hand grenades and talked to the local sheep.

"Hey, Lamb Chops."

"Yo-ho, Woolly Bum!"

"Who knit your sweater, Baa-baaa!"

Charlie tried to interview a cow on his tape re-corder, but the beast stared at him blankly and re-fused to say moo. Bonnie wondered if its tongue had been made into sandwiches. As for Muldoon, an alien creature with sticking-up ears popped out of the ground and made him run for his life. Being a town dog, he'd never seen a rabbit before.

"Yaaaa, you chicken, Muldoon," jeered the Sweet kids.

When they got back, everything had been laid out for eating and Miss Amy had made a daisy chain for Bonnie.

"I thought Lulubelle would like it," she said. "Where is she, anyway? I thought she would enjoy a picnic."

"Hiding," said Bonnie. "Where nobody will never, ever find her even if they look until she's very old."

"She's old already," said Charlie.

"She's not old."

"We'll find her when she falls asleep," said Charlie, "because she snores."

"She doesn't *snore*."

"Swimming pool!" screeched Zoe.

"And anyway," Bonnie added in a grown-up way, "she can't snore, because she's only a doll, and she can't pick her nose either, so there."

Charlie decided to say no more. Whether Lulubelle snored or not, he knew where she was right now and Bonnie didn't. She was in that clock on the landing. He got out his tape recorder and taped a wasp that suddenly came to the picnic.

When they had finished eating, Zoe supervised the clearing-up operation because she believed in a clean environment. Then they went back to the house, bringing most of the square tongue sandwiches with them.

"Perhaps Gertrude will eat them," said Amy. "I do hate waste."

The Sweet kids were helping Amy to dunk her hanging baskets in the kitchen sink when Gerty appeared with a terribly pained expression on her face. (Muldoon slipped quietly out of the kitchen as soon as he set eyes on her.)

"Ooh, do I wish I had wings! My poor feet are killing me!"

"You should have taken a taxi from the village, Gertrude."

"Not me, dear. I'm not one to waste other people's money when I have the two legs the good Lord gave me. Did you have a nice picnic?"

"Oh yes, it was lovely. There are some tongue sandwiches left over if you're hungry."

"Square ones," added Zoe.

"Not me, dear. Them and corned beef don't agree with me. By the way, have you been moving the furniture?"

"No," said Amy. "Why do you ask?"

"Well, I've just walked past the parlor, and the lounge-sofa isn't there anymore."

Frowning, Amy went to see for herself. The sofa had certainly disappeared. So had the two fine bronzes that sat on the mantelpiece. And the long brass fireplace fender with all the hearth irons. Amy's hand shook as she clutched the ruby brooch at her throat.

"Charlie, look in the front room. Is the writing bureau there? It has solid-silver candlesticks on top of it."

After a few seconds Charlie returned with the news.

"Nope. It's gone and so are the candlesticks. We've been done."

"Done?"

"He means we've been burgled, Miss Amy," said Zoe.

"The attic," Amy said breathlessly, seizing Zoe's hand and shaking it. "Check the attic for me, child. Quickly!"

Knowing exactly what she meant, Zoe sprinted up the two broad flights of stairs to the twist in the upper landing. One glance into the attic confirmed that the big glass bottle had been stolen and so had the elephant's foot. Had the robbers got their evil hands on little Bobbie, too?

No! Zoe spotted her huddled in a corner. The awful spiky hair—snipped off so that she could be sold as a boy sweep—made her look like a human brush. What a pity, thought Zoe, that you couldn't give a spook a good cuddle.

A tortoise could have passed Zoe as she came down the stairs. What could she possibly say to that old lady? All her friends had died, she had only memories, now even her best furniture was gone and the spooks had been kidnapped. Two of them, anyway. You needed more than a first-aid kit to mend a broken heart.

On the first landing she met Bonnie, who was staring pop-eyed at the empty space where the big grandfather clock used to be. So that was gone too.

"Zoe?"

"What?"

"Are the bugglers jugglers?"

"What?"

"The bugglers have taken Charlie's juggling balls," Bonnie said in a frightened whisper.

"Try harder not to be a complete dope," said Zoe. "Burglars aren't jugglers. Come on, let's break the news."

The news, of course, was bad from start to finish. Amy sat on a hard-backed chair in the middle of the kitchen, saying, "They were my responsibility. I have let them down badly, you know. All they ever asked for, apart from a little conversation now and then, was to be left alone. And I couldn't even manage that."

She was feeling old and useless, Zoe could tell. But it wasn't your fault, Miss Amy, she was about to say, when Bonnie started to howl.

"THE BIG CLOCK IS GONE AND CHARLIE THEY'VE GOT YOUR JUGGLING BALLS BUT I ONLY PUT THEM THERE BECAUSE YOU SAID SHE DOESN'T USE TOILET PAPER AND SHE WANTS TO MARRY A DUCK."

Gerty, who had been quietly trying to make sense of this whole conversation, now gave up with a shake of her head. They'd all gone barmy.

"They haven't got my juggling balls."

"Yes they have, Charlie. I put them in the big clock and they took it away."

"They're in my rubber boots," said Charlie. "I switched them for Lulubelle."

"The doll was in the clock?" cried Zoe.

"Probably still is. She's been kidnapped," said Charlie.

Bonnie had gone completely stiff. Then, on hearing the word "kidnapped," she threw herself sideways and began to beat the living daylights out of a flowery cushion. To do this she used her head as well as her hands and feet.

"THEY'VE GOT MY LULUBELLE THEY'VE GOT MY LULUBELLE AND I'LL NEVER SEE MY LULUBELLE

AGAIN," she screeched, assisted by the loyal Muldoon in the hall.

"Look, dear, have a blueberry muffin," said Gerty. "There's no use getting worked up over a silly old doll. It didn't even have a mouth, now, did it? There are plenty more where that old rag came from, I can tell you."

"She did have a mouth," Charlie said fiercely. "She had a new mouth. And she wasn't old, and we liked her."

Bonnie stopped crying. She stopped because she couldn't believe her ears. She had never known this before—that Charlie liked Lulubelle.

The phone rang. "I'll get it, dear," Gerty hurried to say. "That'll be my sick mother."

"Well," sighed Amy, pressing herself out of the chair, "let's not be too downhearted. That is always very important in life. Perhaps if we make a list of the things that are missing, we can think of what to do next."

When the others went out of the kitchen, Zoe decided to make herself useful by tidying away the remains of the picnic. Everything went into a trash can except for the leftover sandwiches, which she put into the fridge. And that was when she noticed something that didn't quite fit.

The tongue sandwiches—the ones that Gertrude Moag had said she didn't like *twice*—weren't there.

10...

Clues

The police arrived.

Well, he was actually only one policeman—Bill Partridge's grandson, also called Bill. Amy remembered pushing him through the village in his baby carriage.

"Good afternoon, ma'am," he said. "If I may take down the particulars."

Perhaps it was the uniform that made him talk funny, Amy supposed, but of course she gave him details of the crime, and Zoe had prepared a list of missing items in the hope that some of them might be traced.

"A heinous crime, burglary, Miss Steadings," Constable Bill Partridge said gravely. "Every thief in the country seems to be at it at the present time."

"They captured Lulubelle and two ghosts," Bonnie chirped, "but they didn't get Charlie's juggling balls or the chimney sweep."

"I should hope not," the constable responded

bravely to this piece of nonsense. "But we're going to get *them*, aren't we, my lovely?"

With a quiet click Charlie's little recorder ran out of tape. Constable Partridge watched him change the cassette, and frowned as if to wonder whether it was legal to make a recording of criminal investigations.

"Rest assured, Miss Steadings, that we shall do everything in our power to apprehend these villains and bring them to justice. Meanwhile, it might not be a bad idea to change your locks. And of course we shall keep you abreast of any developments in the case. Good-bye."

On the way out they passed Gerty in the hall, who plonked down the phone when she saw the policeman and gave a sort of breathless curtsy.

"I must go and slice that cabbage for tea, dear—it won't do not to eat."

Zoe followed her into the kitchen. "How sick *is* your mother, Mrs. Moag?"

"Poorly, dear. It upsets me to talk about her, so run along."

"Did you get your stamps?"

"What stamps?"

The stamps you said you were going into the village for, thought Zoe. "I was just wondering what happened to the tongue sandwiches in the fridge."

"You people ate them."

"No, we ate the square ones. I mean the lovely equilateral triangles with the parsley on top. I guess you ate them yourself, even though they give you heartburn, right?"

"Wrong!" Gerty whacked the cabbage in two with a mighty stroke. "Go and play skipping or something. In my day children were seen and not heard!"

On the way into the garden Zoe wondered about that cabbage, too. Hadn't Gertrude Moag said she would buy a turnip?

She passed Miss Amy with Bonnie on her knee. It was hard to tell which of those two looked more miserable. And what about poor little Bobbie in the west chimney—could a ghost feel lonely? What was Lady Cordelia thinking right now, and snooty old James? He'd have a fit once he realized he'd been stolen. Those robbers had made a really good job of making everybody feel rotten.

Charlie lay on the lawn, playing Muldoon a tape of himself barking at the moon. Everybody was upset but Charlie. It was as if he lived in a different world from other people. She suspected that if Charlie wasn't her brother, she might find a number of things to admire about him.

The recording changed and Bonnie started to howl. *"The big clock is gone and Charlie they've got your juggling balls but I only put them there because you said she doesn't use toilet paper and she wants to marry a duck."*

Zoe squatted beside Charlie, suddenly thinking. She turned off the machine.

"Charlie, are you listening to me?"

"Yeah."

"When you put Lulubelle into the clock, what else did you see in there?"

"Some things all wrapped up and a big gun. I didn't see the lead soldiers, but they must have been there because the spook in the big wide skirt saw the Moag person put them there. I can't figure out why, though."

So Charlie had been thinking too. Why hide things in a grandfather clock? And why make an extra plate of tongue sandwiches when the things gave her heart-burn? Why a cabbage and not a turnip? Did she buy stamps? Had she even left the house at all?

"And was the clock ticking?" Zoe asked.

"Nope. The big pendulum was pushed to one side and all tied up."

Slowly Zoe came to her knees as she imagined the brass pendulum swinging lazily to and fro through all the years, until one day—it was stopped. Deliberately.

"Charlie. Why would you tie up a pendulum?"

"To stop it swinging about."

"And why would you want to stop it swinging about?"

"I don't know."

"I do. If you knew you were going to be moving it!"

Muldoon, stirred by the excitement in Zoe's voice, sat up and scratched murderously at the neat bandage on his right ear.

"Charlie! That Moag woman is in this deep, up to her fat elbows!"

"You're right! The only time we were out of the house, we got done by burglars. She tipped them off."

"But how would she do that, Charlie?"

"By phoning her sick mother."

This had to be a wild guess, of course, but Zoe couldn't help thinking how brilliant it was. It made everything clear.

"So she puts the lead soldiers into her apron pocket, then into the clock, ties up the pendulum and the clock disappears. And the robbers know when to come because she's right here. Come on, Charlie!"

"Where are we going?"

"To search her room for incriminating evidence, of course. And don't say there won't be any, because if criminals never made mistakes none of them would ever get caught, would they? What we need are clues!"

When you are not used to creeping uninvited into the bedrooms of strangers, it can be quite an ordeal to do so for the first time. Charlie took off his shoes in case the floorboards creaked, while Zoe nibbled at her bottom lip and reminded herself that they were dealing with dirty rotten crooks and so had every right to be fighting on the side of justice. However, only Muldoon was really at his ease. He picked a fight with a pink slipper, for experience had taught him that slippers never fight back.

"Charlie! Look what I've found under the window," whispered Zoe.

She'd found some ivy clippings.

"What do those prove?"

"I don't know, but they might fit into the overall scheme of things. Muldoon, you moonbeam, leave that slipper alone!"

There was nothing in the wardrobe but clothes. A suitcase rattled when Zoe dragged it from under the bed, but there was only a hairbrush inside. From the bedside table a boy within a silver frame smiled out at Charlie.

"There's a book here," he said. "It says *Antiques and How to Recognize Them*."

"Oh, well done!" Zoe flicked through the pages. "This proves she knew what to steal; it'll be good evidence in court. Muldoon!"

Muldoon had just bolted under the bed. In spite of the bandage over his ear there was nothing wrong with his hearing. And he had heard the dreadful fall of footsteps outside the bedroom. Hardly had Zoe replaced the book on the bedside table when she turned and saw Gertrude Moag's large frame filling the doorway.

"And what the devil are you two snoopers doing in my bedroom, may I ask?"

Seeing those fat folded arms and those quivering chins, Zoe almost blurted out the truth even though she knew what a disaster this could be; but Charlie spoke up.

"We're looking for our dog. He got lost."

"Dog! That unclean brute is in *here* to piddle all over the place?"

Gertrude Moag glanced down, saw her beaten-up slipper, spotted the tip of snout poking out from under the bed, and smiled, showing her teeth.

"Come on out, my little pet. Gerty wants to show a bad little doggy-woggy what happens when he won't do what he's told."

Muldoon, who was no fool, passed her like a dark brown blur, followed smartly by Charlie and Zoe.

"And if I see that fleabag in here again, he's gonna need *real* bandages!" cried Gertrude Moag.

Although her heart was beating much more quickly than it should have been, Zoe paused at the door to speak her mind as calmly as she could.

"You're not a very polite person, Mrs. Moag," she said.

"POLITE? I'LL POLITE YOU!" This mighty cry pursued them down the stairs.

In the garden, deep among the lupins, they found Muldoon. He seemed pleased enough to see them, but had to be coaxed into the daylight after his narrow escape from death upstairs. As Zoe removed his ear bandage, the poor old dear's heart thumped so madly that she gave him a strong cuddle.

"Okay, Charlie, this means war. Fleabag, indeed! How are we going to nail her and stick her in jail for ten million years and a day?"

Quite unexpectedly, Charlie came up with an answer immediately.

"There is a way, but we'll have to stake out the phone."

"You mean listen in? But how?"

"Tape her." Charlie switched on his recorder and spoke into his palm. "Criminal Investigation Tape Number One, Side One. Charlie Sweet, Recording Engineer. Chief Suspect phones Sick Mother."

11 ...

Fire!

What a frightful situation to be in, thought Lady Cordelia McIntyre—to wake up somewhere else entirely different from where you thought you were, from where you jolly well ought to be, and not know how you got here! How awful to be so thoroughly helpless and . . . and *insubstantial*. She steered her graceful Presence toward a window (for light is always the best camouflage for a ghost) and looked around her.

Well, perhaps it wasn't too much of a shock. One way and another Cordelia had spent most of her two hundred years surrounded by old things (including, unfortunately, Sir James Walsingham), and this place clearly was no exception. On all sides she saw relics of other days around her: muskets, bed warmers, stuffed owls, quaint clothes and clogs, even a ship's cannon which had surely once belonged on the deck of a stately man-of-war. In this place there were such mountains of rugs, lamps, books, pictures and furniture that she might well have been in a gigantic attic—except that one did not find fireplaces in attics, of course. And this place was jam packed with them. Good gracious, how could it have become the fashion to collect such ugly things? It had always been a rule of hers to stay as far away from sooty objects as possible.

Here and there she noticed some familiar things: pictures from Hungryhouse Lane, and the sofa, and Amy's grand old clock. The carboy, too. Should she wake James and talk to him about the predicament they were in? Not yet, she decided. He would huff and puff and take snuff and say something silly like, "I'll knock someone's block off, Cordelia—I'm no Englishman if I don't."

Above the rumble of traffic from the street outside, she heard voices. A lady had come through the door, to be met by a man whom Cordelia hadn't even noticed.

"Good afternoon, madam, Alexander the Grate at your service. How may I help you?"

"Well, I'm looking for a wartime fireplace, late nineteen-thirties or early forties. One with tiles up the sides. Do you know the sort?"

"We are expert in period pieces, madam, step this way. Redecorating, are we? Oh yes, those old wartime fireplaces—so much atmosphere! Dame Vera

Lynn on the wireless and flying ducks on the wall.
Très bijou . . ."

Oh, dear me, thought Cordelia, it's a shop. People
actually *buy* these things. I could wake up *sold.*

Perhaps she should condense her vapory form into
dear old Rajah's foot and simply hope for the
best. . . . Who was he, anyway, that Alexander person with the spectacles around his neck on a pink
string?

The answer was: a thief, of course. Amy would
never sell them. She must have been robbed. One of
her great fears had come true.

Then James appeared, all of a quiver.

"Cordelia! The fellow's a bounder and a horse
thief! Where are we? In a fix, by jove—what?"

"We're in some kind of shop, James."

"A shop? This isn't a *shop,* it's a graveyard for old
fireplaces. I tell you, Cordelia, this might very well
suit that lower-class sweep with her blasted brushes,
but no ghost from good society could close his eyes
here. Not for a moment. Never!"

The lace hanky fluttered like a panicking insect
throughout this speech, indicating that James would
never be happy until they gave him a room to haunt
in Buckingham Palace.

"Amy's grandfather clock isn't an old fireplace,"
Cordelia pointed out quietly. "It's been stolen."

"You mean they were after *us?*"

"If they were after us, why would they take the clock, James? And all the other things from Hungryhouse Lane?"

"To be sure of getting you and me, of course! They knew we lived in that house somewhere. Now do you see, Cordelia—we've been kidnapped!"

Dear me, sighed Lady Cordelia. How could she point out to James, without being cruel, that he really wouldn't be terribly useful to anyone?

"They don't even know that we are here, James, so please be calm and try to think sensibly about the situation we find ourselves in."

"Calm? Have you looked out the window? Have you seen those car things in the street? Do you realize, Cordelia, that the noble horse is probably extinct? If that's progress, let them hang me high in the morning, by Harry!"

Having whipped himself into a froth of excitement, James floated airily toward the ceiling, sniffing snuff up his nose as he went and fluttering the lace hanky at his wrist as if he were waving this too-cruel world good-bye.

Exactly as I foresaw, thought Cordelia. James had no head for a crisis. And she was about to tell him so when something rather unbelievable happened. A cheeky little monkey with a tail twice as long as itself appeared on the left shoulder of Sir James Walsingham. It was dressed in a suit and hat and seemed like

a cute little thing, really, although James didn't think so.

"Aaaaa! What is it? Get the rotter off me. Where did it come from? By Harry, Cordelia, it's a squirrel wearing *clothes*."

"That is not a squirrel, James. It's a monkey."

It did not matter that Sir James had never seen a monkey, for he hated all furry animals everywhere with the passion that some people reserve for spiders and snakes. He flapped, he quaked, he cried, "Shoo-shoo-shoo, you little beast," until the monkey realized that he might have picked a more friendly shoulder to land on. Cordelia watched the little imp jump up to the ceiling, where his ghostly outline passed through a round, white object.

And now there occurred one of the most extraordinary things Cordelia had ever seen in her life—or since her life had ended, for that matter. This white object—which was about the size of a dinner plate—suddenly began to shriek and wail. The loudness of the noise was bad enough, but the unearthly weirdness of it filled Cordelia with a kind of awe, and for some reason she recalled the dying squeals of a great bull elephant she had once seen felled by marksmen in the Punjab.

Nothing could prevent James from wildly drawing his sword, although once the weapon had cleared the scabbard, he had no idea where to point it.

"By Harry, Cordelia, I think we're up against something jolly devilish this time, what?"

On the shop floor below, there was panic too. The lady bolted from the shop. That man who called himself Alexander ran to the phone and began to shout into it.

"FIRE! All my lovely stuff, quick! Seventeen Frogworth Place. SEVENTEEN, are you deaf? Oh, mother of mercy, I'm not insured. QUICK!"

After thumping down the phone, he ripped a red cylinder from the wall and staggered about the room with it. However, like James and his sword, he didn't seem to know where to point it. From time to time he sniffed the air, like a dog.

Abruptly the noise stopped.

"Chap's gone clean mad!" muttered James. "I once saw a fellow go like that after he'd eaten some dodgy mushrooms. I say, Cordelia, here come two chappies in yellow helmets. You don't suppose we're in some kind of theater, by any chance?"

"Be careful, James, they're looking up here. Whatever has happened, I'm sure it has something to do with that little white thing on the ceiling. That monkey made it sound off."

The two men in helmets began to search the shop, paying particular attention to the fire burning under the big chimney. At last they seemed satisfied. One even took off his helmet, revealing a bald patch underneath. James mumbled something about recommending a good wig maker in the Strand.

"There's no fire here, sir. We can't find anything for you to worry about."

"But it went off, I tell you! All my customers heard it, they had to abandon the shop."

"Some smoke alarms are like that. May I suggest that you have it replaced by a more expensive model? And it might be best, sir, if you didn't keep a fire burning in that grate for the time being."

"But I'm Alexander the Grate. My customers like to see a living fire. I sell fireplaces."

"Suit yourself, sir. Only—please—no more false alarms, eh?"

"I'll have it replaced this very day!"

When the men had gone, Alexander the Grate (such a name to be born with, thought Cordelia) replaced the red cylinder on the wall and then proceeded to rake the fire until nothing remained of it but dull ashes.

"Well, I don't know," muttered James. "You can thrash me with a riding crop if I understand what's going on."

"It's called progress, James," said Cordelia brightly. "Who would have thought they'd invent a *smoke* alarm! And how fascinating that we know how to set it off! Something tells me, James, that someone is going to be very sorry that he ever set foot in a place called Hungryhouse Lane."

12...

Tick Tock, Look in the Clock

But who the devil are you, sir?" cried James. "Who are you, I say? What? Where did you come from? And is that beast on your shoulder really necessary?"

The Presence whom James was now addressing on the upper gallery of the antique shop didn't seem in the least put out by the display of aristocratic fury in front of him. Indeed, he chuckled deeply as he stroked the underside of his monkey's chin.

"This here's no beast, your lordship," he said. "This be Admiral Foo-Foo, our ship's monkey. Sure, many a tot of rum the admiral and I had from the same pint pot. It's Irish I am! Captain Henry John Blackskull. And may I say," he added with a sly glance at Cordelia, "that it's a whale of a pleasure to be addressing a woman of quality. I'm thinking it's a great pity, my lady, that we never met while we had flesh."

Cordelia didn't think it was a pity at all, but she

supposed that he meant well. Evidently this curious ex-human being lived in the old ship's cannon she had seen earlier. He looked quite handsome in a three-cornered hat and a long frockcoat, but the pistol and the sword tucked into the leather band around his waist made one wary of him. Captain Henry John Blackskull wasn't the sort one might meet strolling through Piccadilly or the Vauxhall Gardens. And good heavens, those earrings!

"But what do you *do*?" cried James.

"*Did*, sir," came the reply. "With respect to your lordship, my doing days are done. Why, I brought brandy for the parson! I chased Spanish treasure and English gold on each of the seven seas—I lived for months on end off octopus and turtle! The price on my head made a fellow proud to be so valuable. Many a time I was tempted to turn myself in for the reward."

James could contain himself no longer. As a law-abiding English gentleman, he was positively writhing with disgust.

"The fellow's a pirate! You're a pirate, sir! Demme, Cordelia, he's a cutthroat from the taverns. A pirate, I say! With a . . . a . . . a *squirrel*."

Neither Blackskull nor his "squirrel" seemed offended by this outburst.

"Quite honestly, James," said Cordelia, "I don't think it matters what he is, after all this time." She glanced up at the round white plate fixed to the ceiling, the one that had caused all that earlier panic and confusion. "Tell me, Captain Blackskull, could I borrow Admiral Foo-Foo for a while? There's something I'd rather like him to do. . . ."

Later that morning, just before noon, Alexander the Grate closed his shop in Frogworth Place and marched down Main Street like a man with something serious on his mind. People on the sidewalk got out of his way when they saw the expression on his face—the kind of expression that may have appeared from time to time on the faces of Cleopatra's food tasters. And the ends of his silk necktie swirled behind him like a couple of frisky pennants.

The sour taste in Alexander's mouth was due to the fact that his second smoke alarm had just gone off for no reason. Fuming, he swept through the door of Domestic Appliances Ltd.

"Can I help you, sir?"

"I want to speak to the manager of this shifty outfit about a smoke alarm."

"Didn't we just fix . . ."

"Yes, you did fix—an hour ago. It went off for no reason."

"Are you sure there was no smoke, sir?"

"Yes, I am. Are you sure your electrician is qualified to use a screwdriver?"

An engineer returned to the shop with Alexander, where he replaced the second smoke alarm with a third smoke alarm, free of charge. It was the very latest thing in smoke alarms, the engineer said before he left. He'd been gone five minutes when the third smoke alarm went off.

Wildly, Alexander the Grate stared up at the third smoke alarm to go berserk in three hours. There it was, full of sound and fury, having a wail of a time. He wanted to throw something heavy at it, but nothing lay to hand. Besides, he still had enough presence of mind to realize that he would probably miss, so he made a beeline for the phone instead. What he saw floating there made him forget all about smoke alarms.

It was a ghost. No two ways about it. A ghost. You could see through the horror's waistcoat to the telephone beyond. "Aah, sugar me!" Alexander said, or something like that, as his legs brought him to a halt. I'm having a visitor, he thought, from beyond the grave.

Being an antiques dealer, Alexander was familiar with the various periods of English history. That wig, those buckled shoes, that hanky at the wrist, that sword . . . One part of his mind whispered ever so quietly: It's George the Third. The other part, a much bigger part, started to make a noise that any smoke alarm would have been proud of.

"You're a bounder and a thief, sir. By Harry, I say you are no Englishman!" the specter cried, whipping out his sword.

Alexander would have preferred to have fainted clean away; but, somehow drawing strength from he knew not where, he seized a mighty poker, with which he carved great whistling slices through the air. For the most part his eyes were closed as he did this. When he opened them again, he found that he had whacked the phone under the antlers of a nearby moose and reduced a rosewood table to firewood.

But thankfully, George the Third was gone.

Within minutes, the shop was closed. Alexander parked himself in a corner of the King's Head Pub on Main Street, where he talked to himself over a double brandy.

This is all in your head, Alex, he said. You've eaten something, sailor—no more anchovies for breakfast, that's for sure. It's Shredded Wheat from here on in.

Maybe I was asleep. Was I? Mother of Mercy, George the Third!

In the afternoon Alexander returned to his shop in a more constructive frame of mind. His nerves were on edge, that's all—most likely the blasted cold he'd caught while yachting had given him a temperature. Overheated brains often saw visions. After swallowing a couple of aspirin he pulled down his blinds, sank into a Victorian leather chair and ordered his brain to take a rest. Indeed, he even allowed himself a little smile. George the blooming Third. Whoever next?

After a time he seemed to dream that he was floating on the sparkling water of his swimming pool in Rio, and Gerty was back in England living in an old-age home. But wait! A beautiful lady swirled out of the light to whisper sweetly in his ear. . . .

"Tick tock, look in the clock," she said. And again, "Tick tock, look in the clock. Look in the clock." What super jewelry she had! Alexander could almost swear that she wore a Queen Anne necklace; but when he reached out to touch, his fingers passed clean through her slender throat. With a strangled cry he came awake, heart thumping, watching and listening for he knew not what.

The faintest of sounds came to him now, quiet and regular: *tick tock, tick tock, tick tock*. Weird, how such a tiny sound seemed to swell and fill the room, as a whisper can fill a cathedral. *Look in the clock, look in the clock.* The grand old timepiece he'd stolen from Hungryhouse Lane seemed to beckon him from the far wall.

What a masterpiece in walnut, Alexander was thinking as he approached it. None of your modern digital trash here—this work of art was a celebration of time itself, and far too good for a senile old bird on her last legs who probably never looked at it from New Year's Eve to Christmas. Yes, beautiful things belong with those who know how to appreciate them, thought Alexander as he opened the little door to look inside. I *deserve* this clock, and it deserves me.

The pendulum swung to and fro. But the pendulum was not alone. There was a head in there. Just a head. Each swing to and each swing fro passed through the wig of George the Third, who smiled up at him and winked with an empty eye.

Oh, sugar! Alexander clapped a shaking hand to his own ticker, which seemed to be lurching to and fro with each mighty throb.

"Sir James Walsingham at your service, sir! I understand that you are having trouble with your jolly old smoke alarms."

13...

Chief Suspect
Phones Sick Mother

All the Sweet kids sat on Charlie's bed.

Except for the four-legged Sweet, who was deep asleep, they talked quietly to one another like a gang of spies. After all, the enemy's bedroom was just a few steps down the corridor.

On the covers lay a number of the little cassettes that Charlie used in his recorder.

Zoe was becoming impatient with her brother, the sound engineer. So far, they'd listened to Ghost Interview side one, a wasp at a picnic, a dumb cow, Lulu-belle in the bath with Jaws, a clicking grasshopper, and Constable Bill Partridge.

"Charlie—did you get her or didn't you? Where is Chief Suspect Phones Sick Mother?"

"Hang on, I got 'em mixed up."

It hadn't been easy, the bugging of Chief Suspect's telephone calls. For a start they'd had to watch the phone for three hours, during which time she hadn't

made any calls. Then came a stroke of luck. Somebody phoned *her* and the clever plan went into
action. Just as the Chief Suspect picked up the phone,
Charlie walked forward with a posy of sweet pea in
a little wicker basket and set it on the shelf beside the
phone.

"This is a private call, sweetie."

"Miss Amy wants these flowers here."

"Get lost."

"Up your nose," Charlie said as he got lost. Hidden
by the sweet pea, his recorder was taping away.

But maybe the plan had run into some sort of
difficulty, thought Zoe. The batteries could have
given up the ghost, or perhaps Chief Suspect
wouldn't speak loudly enough to be heard and Zoe's
stroke of genius (the sweet pea) might be wasted.

Maybe there even *was* a sick mother.

"What is keeping you, Charlie?" she demanded to
know.

"I think I've got it. It must be this one here."

"Do you think we'll hear them?"

"We might get Chief Suspect," said Charlie. "But
Sick Mother's voice probably won't be loud
enough."

With a click the tape began to run. They heard
Chief Suspect telling Charlie to get lost, and Charlie
saying, *"Up your nose."*

"That's very rude!" Bonnie said loudly.

"Shhh!"

"No, *Alexander, I wasn't telling you to get lost, just one of the local pests. Although don't you think it's a bit late to be calling? You sound a bit hoarse, dear. I sincerely hope you're taking Knox's Oval Lozenges for that throat. What? A smoke alarm? . . . Three smoke alarms? . . . Alexander, have you been drinking? There is no such thing as a . . . You thought he was George the WHO? What do you mean, that's not all? This is enough moonshine for one night, if you ask me. . . . Alex, how could she float like a bubble, and I don't care if she was wearing a Queen Anne necklace, you'll have to pull yourself together, don't you dare go feebleminded on me, boy, or you'll ruin everything. One more load and . . . I don't understand what you're saying, Alex dear. Who are Long John Silver and Admiral Foo-Foo? What? Tick tock, look in the clock? Only its head, I see. I see. Well, why didn't you give it a thick ear and knock the stupid smile off its face, then? And stop saying 'Good-bye Rio,' it doesn't make any sense. Look. Stay right there. I'll be around first thing in the morning, and we'll soon see about spooky-wookies!"*

The phone went dead, the recorder went click, and the Sweet kids celebrated by bouncing about on the bed and thumping pillows.

"Sick Mother is a man!" cried Charlie.

"Shh!" hissed Zoe.

Muldoon, horrified to discover that he'd gone to

bed on a trampoline, jumped to the floor and rushed about impressively. Then Zoe disappeared in search of a phone book.

"Does this mean that Lulubelle is coming back?" Bonnie asked Charlie.

"Yep. Thanks to my modern technology."

Now that Lulubelle was about to be recaptured, a tear or two brightened Bonnie's lovely eyes. She may have been feeling guilty for some of the terrible things she had done in her lifetime.

"Charlie?"

"What?"

"Would you like me to make satin bows for your juggling balls?"

"What?"

"I could make satin bows and I could tie them around the middle. Miss Amy says I can tie bows as nice as ninepence."

Charlie may well have been thinking, Juggling balls don't wear satin bows, you daft moonbeam, but for some reason he didn't say so. He just said, "I forget where I put them."

Now Zoe returned, whooping quietly but in triumph. "He's in the phone book, right? Under Moag, of course. I bet he's her husband and they're in this together. Here's what it says: Alexander Moag, Antiques Dealer, Seventeen Frogworth Place. Then I looked it up in the Yellow Pages and you'll never guess what he calls himself: *Alexander the Grate, Specialist in Period Fireplaces*." With a mighty thud, Zoe closed the book and cried, "Come on!"

"Where are we going?" asked Bonnie.

"Up to the attic. We have to talk to Bobbie. Alexander the Grate, indeed! We're going to show that gangster something that'll put him off fireplaces for *life*!"

Breakfast in Hungryhouse Lane was a strange affair.

The three Sweet kids sat at the table around a communal plate of overdone toast. From time to time they stared at the gangster's wife in the plastic apron who was making tea for Miss Amy at the cookstove. Amy Steadings sat up very straight in a highbacked chair and said, "You really needn't go to any trouble on my account, Gertrude, for I have quite lost my appetite this morning."

"Now, now, now," clucked Gerty. "We must eat, mustn't we? And I'm going away today, and who knows when you'll get a proper cooked meal again, dear?"

"We're getting Lulubelle back today," Bonnie piped up, only to be thumped on the left thigh by her sister and whacked on the right arm by her brother. In normal circumstances she would have screamed blue murder.

"How sick *is* your mother?" Zoe asked, nibbling innocently on a piece of toast.

"Didn't have a good night, the poor duck. But it comes to us all, doesn't it? That's what I always say: it comes to us all. And now I must fly. There's only the nine-thirty bus into town. Cheers, my dears."

"Cheers," said Charlie.

Breakfast continued in silence until Muldoon trotted into the kitchen as if he owned the joint. Obviously, the coast was now clear.

"I really can't believe it of Gertrude, you know," Amy Steadings muttered sadly. "It's too bad."

"I'll phone for the taxi," said Zoe.

"Don't you think we should perhaps get in touch with Bill Partridge's grandson? There might be trouble, children."

"Naw, cops wouldn't understand about the spooks," said Charlie.

"And anyway," Zoe pointed out, "I'm bringing my first-aid kit in case anyone needs a bandage or a tourniquet."

The red first-aid case was one of the first things the taxi driver saw when he pulled in front of the grand old house. He also saw an elderly woman, a mongrel with its tongue hanging out sideways, and three children—the eldest of whom carried an object that might have been a cage with a blanket thrown over it. This cage was almost as big as herself.

"This is a very tiny little car," said Bonnie as she

climbed in. "Daddy's car is twice as big as this car. Charlie can juggle in Daddy's car, can't you, Charlie?"

"It'll have to do," said Zoe, shoving in the big birdcage she'd found in the attic. "Driver, we're going to London. Do you know where Seventeen Frogworth Place is?"

"Yeah. I know where everywhere is."

"Put the pedal to the metal, then," said Charlie.

"Look, mate, don't let that dog scratch my seats."

"Our dog is a very experienced traveler," Zoe pointed out as Muldoon licked the driver's ear like a lollipop. "Are you all right, Miss Amy? Let me fix your seat belt. Have you got enough room?"

"Yes. Oh, but did I pull the front door behind me? I think I must have."

They were on their way. The taxi driver began to hear strange snippets of conversation that made him wonder about the passengers in his car. "I'm going to give Lulubelle a new mouth," said the littlest one. "A nice smily-mouth with turny-up ends." The boy whipped out a tape recorder and whispered peculiar phrases like "chief suspect" and "sick mother" and "save the spooks." The oldest girl talked about Alexander the Great as if he was living down the road instead of being dead for a couple of thousand years.

Bunch of crackpots, thought the driver. After some minutes, he asked, "What's in the cage, then?"

"You wouldn't believe me if I told you," said Zoe.

"Why is it covered by a rug?"

"That's not a rug, it's a blanket."

"It's a parrot, right?"

"Yes, it's a parrot."

"Is your parrot sick, then?"

"No. It got stuck up a chimney."

"What can it say?"

"It doesn't talk."

"What use is a parrot that can't talk?"

"Actually, if it could talk, it would say: Mind your own business."

"Excuse me for breathing, sweetheart," said the taxi driver, switching on his radio.

Before long they had left Hungryhouse Lane, Tunwold village and the quiet country far behind, and were approaching the city along a busy highway.

"I wonder what makes her do it?" Amy Steadings said suddenly. "What is it that brings out the wickedness in people? Gertrude was quite kind in her own rough way, you know."

"She's a rip-off artist," said Charlie. "One more load and they'd have disappeared into the underworld where no crook ever squeals on another crook and we'd have lost them instead of catching them red-handed."

"Oh dear," sighed Amy. The taxi came to a halt, and they got out.

"Thirty-one pounds, please," said the driver.

"Thirty-one POUNDS!" Zoe almost exploded. "You can't be serious—we don't carry that sort of money around on our persons."

"Oh, I get it! Fare dodgers, eh? I knew there was something fishy about you lot."

"How dare you! Our dad could buy your whole taxi with the interest on his capital investments," cried Zoe.

"Ten taxis," said Charlie.

"And he could buy me a helicopter for my birthday," Bonnie threw in for good measure.

"I think I have the money here," said Amy Steadings. "Oh dear, yes. It's here somewhere."

As he waited, the taxi driver stared at the Sweet kids, plus their dumb parrot and their red first-aid case, as if they had just beamed down from a passing starship. When the old lady coughed up the money, he took off like a Formula One racing driver. Zoe hoped that he didn't have an accident and therefore require her medical assistance one day.

And there it was on the sunny side of the street: number 17. ALEXANDER THE GRATE sparkled in golden letters on a maroon background. The Sweets were filled with excitement as they stared at it between the passing vehicles, for in there were Lady Cordelia McIntyre and Sir James Walsingham, and Chief Suspect and Sick Mother—not to mention many of Miss Amy's most precious things.

"We're here Bobbie," Zoe whispered to her sick parrot. "The time has come for you to do your stuff. Let's see what happens when Alexander finds *you* in his grate!"

14...

A Bandage for Gertrude

Alexander, surrounded by grates, paced around the floor of his shop in ever-diminishing circles until he came to a complete stop. And when he came to the stop, he threw out his arms as if to warn an invisible orchestra that their moment had come.

Then the arms flopped to his sides. Harmlessly.

"It is *not* some jerk of a joker, Mother. I saw it with my own two eyes as well as I'm seeing you now. It was right there *inside* the clock, it winked at me with an empty eye and spoke to me on the subject of smoke alarms. He says we stole him from Hungry-house Lane."

Moonshine! thought Gerty. But she bustled forward, determined to be full of jolly good cheer. There was nothing new in all this, actually—her Alex had always been a little bit nervous and high-strung. Such a great reader of monster and horror comics, he was!

"You're run-down, dearie, that's all. Why, there's

nothing in that old clock but the pendulum and that tatty old doll. There wouldn't be room for a ghost in there, Alexander, would there, duck? Not if you think about it."

For most of the night Alexander had been thinking about it, and now he was on the point of losing his temper, as people who are under pressure often do. He wanted to say, Listen, you old cow, it's a ghost and the pendulum passed right through the middle of its *head*. Ghosts aren't like you or me. The blighters are from beyond the grave and that's what makes them weird and scary.

However, he didn't say that, but instead looked out of the window at the street, where a scruffy mongrel stared in at him from the pavement. Its lollopy tongue stuck out sideways.

"When I go to sleep, the other one comes, you know. If it's not King George, it's Queen Anne. Or Admiral Foo-Foo."

"Who is Admiral Foo-Foo?"

"Long John Silver's monkey, Mother."

String me up, thought Gerty, now he's seeing monkeys.

"Alex—you will pull yourself together!" barked Gerty. "The house is a gold mine. Just one more run and we can take a long rest far away from here. We might even be able to buy you a bigger boat and sail away to Ireland."

Alexander blinked at the word "Ireland." He seemed to be thinking of somewhere else.

"Yacht, Mother. I do not sail boats."

"You'll sink like a blasted stone if you don't listen to me! Think of all the goodies we've got already. That musket might have been fired by Cromwell himself, you know. I looked it up in my book of—"

At that moment Gerty broke off, for she had just noticed white fragments on the floor. Had something priceless been broken?

"My smoke alarm," Alexander explained. "It went off at four in the morning. A policeman, a police car, three nightwatchmen and a tramp turned up at my door."

"How did it get broken?"

"I belted it with a brass candlestick, that's how!" cried Alexander. "That's one dead smoke alarm, may the blighter rest in pieces!"

Sure enough, Gerty found the candlestick—an Edwardian work whose beautiful ornamental branches had obviously come off during the assault on the smoke alarm. Stone me, thought Gerty, this business is getting out of hand. She glanced at the raked ashes under the big chimney. Was Alexander cracking up completely?

"But your fire isn't lit, dear. There was no smoke."

"The fire's got nothing to do with it. Admiral Foo-Foo does it with his *tail*."

Tail my foot, Gerty was thinking—when she realized that something had just come down the chimney. A second glance told her that it wasn't, in fact, a something; it was a some*body*.

Oh, my gawd, thought Gerty. This sure wasn't Father Christmas. Not that Father Christmas wouldn't have been bad enough, but this looked like a ten-year-old sweep! A set of chimney brushes seemed to ooze miraculously through the stone wall and settle on his skinny shoulders.

You're looking at a chimney-sweep ghost, Gerty, a voice within her head seemed to croak.

"It's not! You're some joker in sawn-off jeans and bare feet!"

But Gerty, the voice said—*it's floating.*

"Aah. Oh, my gawd!"

The sooty little hoverer didn't need wings or helicopter blades to just hang there in space. He had his own private means of locomotion. *It's looking right at you, Gerty, out of those spooky black eyes.*

"Don't you eyeball me, you shifty tick, or I'll soon thicken your ear!"

Up rose the phantom brushes in a great slow arc to point straight at Gerty's heart. *But Gerty, your hand will simply pass through its ear, dear. And it's coming to get you. So what are you going to do now?*

"Oh, Alexander," whimpered Gerty. "I think there's a ghost in your grate."

But when she turned, Alexander had company of his own. He grinned at her—well, his lips moved. Frankly, her son looked as though he'd seen a ghost. Which he had, of course. Three of them.

"Mother. Allow me to introduce King George, Queen Anne and Long John Silver. He's a pirate."

Three of them and a monkey. Gerty's head began to swim, and she wondered whether people were right: Could your hair turn white overnight if you got a big fright? For a moment she thought she heard the bark of a dog; and imagined, too, the red outline of a first-aid kit as great rolling waves of panic dragged her under.

There was nothing like a crisis for bringing out the best in Zoe Sweet. She snipped the bandage around Gerty's head with a flourish and spoke calmly to her patient as she tucked away her scissors.

"There. I have applied an antiseptic pad to the wound in your head so that germs can't breed in there. The bandage will hold it in place. You're very lucky I was here to stop the bleeding, or your life might have slowly ebbed away."

Thus satisfied with a job well done, she snapped shut the red lid of her case.

Gerty found herself on the floor, cradled in the arms of Amy Steadings. Although her eyes were wide open, she could not be sure just yet that the world had returned to normal, for the littlest Sweet girl stood close by, hugging her doll as she spoke to the chimney ghost. Who was sitting on the head of a moose.

"Oh, Bobbie, you have saved Lulubelle, you are my favorite spook and you can help me feed my reindeer when I get it for Christmas and you can ride in my helicopter."

And the male Sweet seemed to be holding out a tape recorder to that pirate creature, saying, "Did they ever make you walk the plank?" And that awful King George drifted across her vision at an angle of forty-five degrees. "Gallows too good for 'em, what?" he bellowed, then sniffed the back of his hand.

Gerty twisted to look up into the face of Amy Steadings. "Has my hair turned white, dearie?" she whispered.

"Only the bandage is white, Gertrude. And be still. You hit your head on the fender when you fell."

"It's the first time, ma'am," Gerty went on hoarsely, for she could see the fix she was in. "I've had a hard life, love. His dad run away to sea when he was four. I've seen the down side of life, love, you've no idea. And he's not a bad boy, my Alex. He's always been so good to his mother."

"That's no excuse for being a crook," said Zoe. "They'll give you ten years each using our evidence, I should think."

"Oh, gawd."

"I don't like to believe ill of anyone, Gertrude," said Amy, "and I am prepared to be lenient if you will promise me never to steal and rob from people again. You will return everything to Hungryhouse Lane, of course, that goes without saying. Today, please."

"Bless you forever, ma'am, you have the heart and soul of a saint."

But Amy was thinking sadly of Cordelia, who had just condensed her Nonmaterial Presence into the elephant's foot. What her dear friends needed now was a period of Unwakeful Serenity, not more questions and excitement and publicity.

Saintliness had nothing to do with it.

15...

Praise for the Parents

The holiday break for Mr. and Mrs. Sweet was almost over, and really, it was quite amazing how much they had missed their children about the house. Games of backgammon were played without interruption. They ate out at fancy restaurants. They got up in the morning when it suited *them*. Friends whom they had invited over for the evening actually did come over when it was established that the Sweet kids wouldn't be there. And no dog hairs over the carpet and furniture! sighed Mrs. Sweet as the white Rolls rolled through the gates of Hungryhouse Lane.

"I hope they haven't been too bad," she said to Geoffrey.

"I'm filling it in with concrete," Geoffrey swore between clenched teeth. "I am, you know—I really am."

In his mind's eye he pictured the filled-in swimming pool—a constant reminder to his squabbling children of what might have been.

116

They were waiting at the door with Amy Steadings, all packed up and ready to go. Bad sign, thought Geoffrey. That old lady had the heart of a lion, but five days was surely too long, even for her.

As Mr. and Mrs. Sweet disembarked, hugs and kisses were exchanged all around (except for Muldoon, whose tail had been beautifully bound in a white bandage).

"Mommy, Daddy, we found a pirate and a monkey and we brought them home. And look—do you see Lulubelle's new smily-mouth?"

"Her mouth is lovely and smily, pet. Is that a smudge on her face?"

"She got dirty all over when she got captured by baddies."

An extremely dirty look passed from Mr. Sweet to his son as he said, "I hope, Miss Amy, that they have been well-behaved for you?"

"Well-behaved? Mr. and Mrs. Sweet, they have been so wonderful I can hardly wait until their next visit. Your children are a credit to you! And in these difficult times, too, when young people can be so demanding. How on earth do you do it? I am certain that you must be terribly proud of them!"

Mr. and Mrs. Sweet glanced at each other, as if to check that their ears were in working order. In all honesty they felt a little embarrassed, for they did not have much practice in dealing with this kind of praise.

"Well," Geoffrey muttered with a cough. "I hope you enjoyed the VCR."

"But we didn't open the box," said Amy.

"Daddy, believe me, we didn't have time to waste on watching videos," said Zoe. "No way."

Good heavens. How extraordinary, thought Mrs. Sweet. Hugs and kisses were suddenly exchanged once more—this time with promises of letters and phone calls thrown in—then the Sweet kids boarded the Rolls like pirates taking a treasure ship.

They were going home.

Let us fast-forward our story by about fifteen minutes or so, and bring it to a close by pressing the pause button.

In the Sweet Rolls Royce, Mr. Sweet is driving slowly (for him) because his mind is really thinking about the swimming pool. What a good job he hadn't filled in the thing after all!

Mrs. Sweet is wondering: Didn't they watch *any* TV at *all*?

Muldoon, like an experienced traveler, is already fast asleep in spite of his stiff white tail.

Zoe is feeling deeply satisfied that she has probably saved her first life, although she would have preferred to have wasted a bandage on a more useful member of society than a stealer of furniture.

Bonnie is nursing a box in her lap. Charlie doesn't know it yet, but his juggling balls are in the box, each one tied up in a gorgeous satin bow. This is his reward for loving Lulubelle.

In the west chimney little Bobbie is giving Admiral Foo-Foo a last cuddle before she withdraws into a state of Unwakeful Serenity. Sir James is listing to starboard again as he cries to anyone who happens to be listening, "Did you see that unspeakable dog scratching itself? It's enough to make a chap feel itchy."

Standing by his cannon, Captain Henry John Blackskull laughs heartily. "A flea wouldn't have much fun on you, Sir Jamesie—there's nothing for it to eat."

The outline of Lady Cordelia McIntyre billows softly in a draft as she smiles and thinks that a pirate might be interesting. Imagine eating octopus and turtle!

Two floors below, Amy Steadings is writing to a distant cousin of hers in Somerset, hoping that she will come and stay with her for the winter. Will Sir James and the new ghost get on together, she wonders?

And in the backseat of the Rolls, Charlie Sweet is speaking into his tape recorder. "Criminal Investigation Tape, Side Two. Recording Engineer, Charlie Sweet. Saved the spooks. Got the stupid doll back. Case closed."